THE DEATH OF HOPE

Book Three of the trilogy:

"It's The Human Condition"

The Death of Hope by Ian Waters

ISBN 9798876121660

For the future generation:

Ariana Georgia, Aelyn Sophia, Leo Anthony

And Luca Giovanni

CONTENTS

RETRIBUTION DAY

One

The barman glanced up at the wall clock as he polished another pint glass. Half an hour to go, he thought, then the landlord will be down to look after his regulars and prepare for a lock-in with the chosen few. I can have a couple of pints and a pie, then off for a game of snooker. He liked these quiet, Saturday afternoons when Spurs were at home.

He liked the pub even better. A long time ago, he'd imagined himself suited and booted, serving up fancy cocktails in one of London's top hotels, but he soon realized that would never happen. Even with the white shirt, black bow tie and patent leather shoes, he just looked wrong. He didn't fit the image at all, not with a face that was simply too rough for the surroundings. Even when he smiled, he looked threatening. So he'd resigned himself to working in pubs for the rest of his life. Then, as his own drinking took hold, he gradually slid down the scale of pubs in terms of their class and quality. But he was smart enough to recognize and accept that, and he eventually grew to like the rougher, harder end of the business.

And, as he slid further down the ladder, he learned to curb both his fiddling from the till and the careful removal of stock, both of which he had become expert at. He quickly realized that the rougher the pub, the sharper were the landlords. Many places would simply show bent barmen the door, without pay or references but pubs like this one had customers who would dole out beatings as a favour to the landlord. And the severity of said beating usually matched the scale of the fiddling. And while he had no problem drinking himself to death, something he regarded as an inevitability, he had no desire to end up a physically broken man unable to work at all. Thus he gradually became that rarest of beasts, an honest London barman.

He'd been new to the area when he got the job less than two weeks ago, but he'd recognised the pub for what it was as soon as he arrived. At fifty-three and by now seriously into the drink, it fitted him perfectly. It had, like him, seen better days and was a little out of its time. When many of London's pubs, were being tarted up, or completely re-modelled, this one had escaped. He'd felt perfectly at home even before he'd pulled his first pint or considered the odds of trying to fiddle his first fiver from the till.

No wallpaper, plush velvet and imitation mahogany here. In decor it was very much as it had been back in the nineteen thirties. A dark, nicotine-stained, two-bar local with round, wood and iron tables and well-worn lino on the floor. It had escaped so-called progress mainly because it was a privately owned free-house and the major brewers simply weren't interested in it.

He didn't know exactly who did own it, but it hadn't taken him long to realise it wasn't the landlord. Sure, he was the one did all the ordering and the daily running, but it was clear from the customers' attitude towards him, especially where after-hours drinking was concerned, that he wasn't fully in charge. The barman had never been able to identify the real owner, but he was sure he'd never been in the place. He'd developed an eye for people all the years he'd worked pulling pints and he knew he wouldn't have missed him. Whoever it was, though, his presence hung over the place like fine mist.

The pub was thirties-style in other ways, too. It didn't attract much passing trade or many women - except a few well into their sixties who weren't exactly classed as women in those parts. Essentially, it sold only three drinks - bitter, lager and whisky. There was the mandatory Guinness pump but that did just a bit more business than a street whore in Belgravia. There was no fruit machine or jukebox. A few years ago, two companies had tried to force machines in but the hospital and funeral bills they'd had to pay on behalf of their 'salesmen' persuaded them there was more profit to be gained elsewhere.

And apart from the old women, the three drinks were sold largely to three groups of customers. Local hard men, their sons and hangers-on, and the older, local working men. The unattached younger men went to newer, smarter pubs where the better-dressed, good-looking girls went. Each group, and every member of each group knew their place in the hierarchy as surely as medieval serfs did. All of which meant there was never any aggravation in the place. The moment anybody started to act silly, they were immediately shown the door. Some gently, some not.

No aggravation until now, that is. The barman glanced up as the man walked into the bar and looked slowly round. He was somewhere in his early forties and built. He wasn't just big, he had a solid hardness that was definitely not the product of some fancy gym. And a serious face to go with it. A face that invited no questions, never mind arguments. One thing's for sure, the barman thought, nobody's showing this one the door no matter what he does.

The man walked with a slow confidence and the barman took in the double-breasted dark blue overcoat, the dark grey suit, pale blue shirt and plain red silk tie. Finished off with a pair of perfectly polished black brogues. Dressed like the businessman he wasn't, and nobody with any sense would ever mistake him for. Especially since he appeared to be so comfortable in a pub like this, despite the clothing.

His entrance had killed the conversations and one or two of the older men nodded to him without getting any response. He took a long, slow look around but couldn't see who he was looking for and approached the bar. The barman didn't know who the man was, but he'd worked this sort of place in London long enough to recognize trouble when he saw it. And this one looked like he could be serious trouble if he set his mind to it. The barman sighed to himself and waited for what was to come.

"Glenmorangie. Large one," the man said in a surprisingly soft south London accent. His eyes continued to check the place out in the mirror behind the bar. The barman poured him a large malt and started to move away. He knew there'd be no money offered and he certainly wasn't going to ask. The man's voice stopped him.

"I'm lookin' for the boy Watson."

"Sorry," the barman said, "I ain't bin here long. I know all the regular faces but..."

But the man had already lost interest. He took a drink of whisky as he turned away from the bar. One of the locals approached him. A small, scruffy, man in his late fifties who'd been drinking with a small group at the end of the bar furthest from the door.

"Davey," the man said. "Don't remember seein' you in here before. You alright?" Dave Collins nodded, wondering where Charlie Harris had suddenly found the balls to talk to him. And use his first name as well.

"Must have a thirst alright, you come in a place like this," Charlie added. "Bit below your level these days I'd've thought."

He seemed to expect a reply, but Collins just leaned against the bar and looked at him.

"Couldn't help but overhear you're lookin' for young Watson," he finally said.

Collins nodded again before he lit a cigarette, wondering if the old man was ever going to get to the point.

"What d'you want him for, eh? What's your man want with him? Not in your league. Not at all. He's a bit've a silly young boy at times, I know, like a lot of them, but that's all he is. He's alright really, bit silly at times like I said but not really bad... "

"Charlie, Charlie, I'd wanted a bleedin' character reference I would've written t'you formal like. You know?"

Charlie nodded. Said nothing.

"So. He in here or what?"

"Think I saw him a while..."

"Think? You? Need a brain for that, Charlie. Even tryin' to think's dangerous for you."

He poked him in the chest. Hard. And Charlie took a couple of steps back. The men near him moved away and concentrated on their drinks. Conversations had not started up again. If Charlie wanted to get involved with Collins, that was down to him. They certainly weren't going to even look interested.

"So don't try, eh. Just say."

"He's in the back room there, with his mates," Charlie said, looking to the barman for confirmation. The barman studiously ignored him and began to feel sorry for young Watson, whoever he was.

"What's he wearing, Charlie?" Collins asked.

"Jeans an' a Spurs shirt, you can't miss him though, 'cos he's..."

But Collins had already drained his whisky and walked through to the back room. Charlie gulped the remainder of his pint, grabbed his cap and slid out of the door. The landlord had joined his mates at the bar, and the barman looked at him and raised his eyebrows in silent question. He got a shake of the head in return. The barman wondered again who the man was and began to feel even more sorry for young Watson.

Three

When Collins walked into the back room, he saw five boys sitting around a table drinking pints of lager. Only one was wearing a Spurs shirt, a red-headed boy, in his late teens it looked like. The conversation stopped as he entered, and they were all careful not to look at him as he walked over to the table.

"Watson," he said quietly, looking directly at the red head. The boy looked at him but didn't speak.

"Who wants 'im?" another boy asked, either too stupid or too drunk to realise this was different and here was a man not to be messed with. The others just stared into their pints.

"Well, since I'm the one doin' the asking son, it must be me, eh?"

"Oh yeah?" the same boy said. "And who the fuck are you then, you..."

Collins barely seemed to move but the boy's stool went flying and he suddenly found himself flat on his back with a size ten black brogue pressing heavily on his chest, the toe hooked under his chin.

"Nobody you need worry about son - or then again, maybe you do," he said, as he casually flattened the boy's nose and broke his front teeth with his heel.

"If you're gonna be that mouthy you need to be able to back it up, son," Collins said as he wiped the blood off his shoe on the boy's jeans.

"Me! It's okay, you can leave him alone now. It's me, I'm the one you're lookin' for," the red head said as his friend crawled away, blood dripping from his shattered nose. "I'm Watson."

He stood up opposite Collins as his mates quickly downed their pints and helped the bleeding boy through to the other bar and the door to the street. The landlord stopped them at the door and handed one of the boys a twenty-pound note. The boy looked at him, eyebrows raised.

"That's for a taxi, get him to hospital or a doctor, whichever. And to make sure you lot keep your bleedin' traps shut. Got it?"

The boys looked at each other, then nodded and hustled their mate out the door.

Collins turned back to the table and looked at the boy. And could see his legs shaking inside his jeans as he stood in front of the table. Looking terrified. This was no good, he thought. No good at all. Have to calm him down. And quickly. There's been too much nonsense in here already. Fucking Charlie Harris. Nobody else in the place would dare say a thing but word would get around now and the Man would definitely not like that. He hadn't intended it to happen like this at all.

"Sit down, son. Sit down," he said. "And relax will you. I just need a quiet word with you is all. C'mon. Sit down."

Watson sat down, still shaking, as Collins pulled up a stool.

"You're not very sociable, are you?" he asked. "Here's me without a drink and you, your glass's still half full. Mine's a large whisky by the way. Glenmorangie. You won't be needin' another one."

Four

Watson got up and went to the bar. The barman looked up but took his time getting down to him. Watson asked for the whisky and looked pleadingly at the man but just got a, 'you're on your own, son' look in return. He took the glass across to the table and stood there. Collins looked up at him.

"What?" he said.

"Lemonade or anythin'?" Watson asked him.

"I would've said," Collins replied and tapped the table with his index finger. Watson put the drink on the table and sat down opposite.

"What've..." Watson started to say but Collins stopped him with a look. And then just carried on looking. Not menacing and not really staring either. Just looking, without saying a word. Watson stood it for about two minutes and then had to speak, before his heart burst through his chest.

"What's he want, eh? Tell me. What's he want with me? I ain't nobody to him, am I? What'm I supposed to've done, eh? I've not done nothing to him, have I? What's it about? Eh? Tell me. What?"

"Who?" Collins said and took a sip of his whisky.

"Eh?" Watson said, totally thrown.

"What does he want, that's what you asked. 'He', you said, not 'me'. Why didn't you ask what it is *I* want?"

"Ah c'mon. I know who you are... and who you work for. Everybody round here does. We all know you're the man does the heavy business for Mr..."

Collins shook his head. "No. Best you don't say his name son."

The boy coloured and took a mouthful of his pint. His hand shook as he stubbed out his cigarette. He glanced at Collins, took another drink and glanced at him again. Collins wasn't a policeman or a trained interrogator, but there was nothing any one of them could have taught him about the power of silence over words in certain situations. He sat, very still and relaxed, looking directly at the boy. He kept it up, not saying a word and not moving, for the better part of two minutes.

"How was I supposed to know she was his daughter, eh?" he finally managed to blurt out. "She didn't exactly advertise..."

Collins smiled. "See? You did know after all. You didn't even have to think about it. You knew what I wanted to talk to you about all the time. So why'd you have to waste my bleedin' time son?"

"I didn't. I mean I wasn't sure that was what you were here about. Don't know what else it could've been, but... see, I... I mean, she... I didn't..." His voice trailed off as Collins sat forward, leaning towards him across the table. The finger pointing at him looked more threatening than a knife blade.

"Get a grip son. You're making no sense at all."

Watson took a few deep breaths trying to gather himself. "What it was... I didn't mean... she wanted me..." He shook his head, trying to hold himself together.

Collins, sighed, then told him to relax, take a deep breath and tell him what had happened.

"It was stupid really. I was at a club, dancin', Saturday night, with my mates an' she was just this tasty piece of skirt there, with her mates. An' I fancied her. Well, you would, you see her. You must've, must've seen her, she's a cracker. 'Specially dressed for the dancin'. And she was givin' me looks. She was interested. What would you've done?"

"No idea, son. But what I would've done ain't exactly the question here, is it?"

"I know, I know. But how was I supposed to know she was his daughter. Eh? Tell me. How was I supposed to know that. Eh?"

Collins shook his head. "Come on, behave. That ain't good enough. Nowhere near good enough. And you know it. Don't piss me about, son, please."

"I'm not, I'm not. She..."

"Look. I know what it's like. I used to go myself. Christ, it's not changed in fifty years. Yeah, the music's changed and the clothes and stuff, even the places look different, called different names and done out different. Dancehalls died and the clubs took over but basically it's the same now as when my old fella used to go. And it ain't just London, it's everywhere. It's the dancin' and the girls. Apart from posin' in your best gear, you're there for one thing and so are they. And it ain't just to appreciate the bleedin' music."

"I know that, I know..."

"Then you should know it's only a game. A boy's game. Right?" Watson nodded. "Right. And like all games, it's got rules. They ain't written down anywhere but everybody with half a brain knows what they are. And it's your choice son if you stick to them or not. If you do, fine. If you don't, you've got some comin'. In football you're booked or sent off. But this ain't football and there's no ref to protect you."

The boy started to say something, but Collins stopped him again with a pointed finger.

"No, listen to me. Listen, because I know, I know the score. There you are, you and your mates, in the club, you're all dressed, best whistles, the shirts and ties, the shoes, had a few drinks, coupla pills maybe and you think you're somethin' special. A few dances, with a few uglies maybe, a few more drinks and then you see somebody's sister maybe, or daughter, daughter of some well-known name. A well-tasty sort. And you fancy your chances. For a laugh. And why not?"

He took a mouthful of whisky.

"So over you go and ask her, and she gives you a dance. Fine. No problem. A couple or three if you're a good-lookin' boy like you, smart dresser and not too bleedin' drunk and you mind your manners. Again, no problem. She ain't stupid, she knows what you're doin' same as you do. A coupla dances then she's back to her mates and you back to yours at the bar. And that's it. End of story. A few dances and a bit of harmless chat. No harm done and the world's back in its proper place."

"But she wanted..." Watson started to say, then stopped and jumped as Collins slammed his palm down on the table.

"I told you to fucking listen! Because even if she doesn't seem to want to, you finish it, you cut out. Because it's in your own interests to do that, am I right?"

Watson nodded and looked at the floor. Collins almost felt sorry for him. Almost.

"Right. You go back to your mates and say to them all, "Guess who that was I was dancin' with, eh? And she fancies me as well." And they're all laughing - but impressed as well. Naturally. Well, they would be, you bein' the only one who had the balls to go and ask her. Because you're something you, eh? But that's it. A few dances, bit of chat, and a spot of givin' it large with your mates. Been done a thousand times before and will be again. So that's what you do. What you don't do..."

"I didn't..."

"What you don't do," Collins said, ignoring him, "is keep on dancin' with her, then buy her drinks, and then dance with her right 'til the end of the night..."

"But I..."

"... that's what you do with the sorts you do know." He leaned across the table, ticking them off on his fingers. "You know the ones. Your sister's friends. Your mates' sisters, friends of your mates' sisters. Girls you know from where you live. Friends of girls you know. Girls you know at school. That's safe. They're safe. 'Cos you know them, you know all about them. You know all the ones with brothers, with fellas. You know the likely consequences. The ones you don't know, you watch. Right? You watch to see if that guy she danced with twice is with a crew of boys. Christ, in some fucking places, you watch to see if she's not runnin' some crew of girls herself. 'Cos they're the worst. Girls. At least guys know some rules when it all kicks off. The girls don't respect any. You watch to see if one guy comes back every three or four dances, buys all her drinks. You watch them and check them out. That's how you operate. To stay in one piece. You enjoy yourself in a way that means you can enjoy yourself again. It makes sense, it always has. It's called survival, son. Survival. It doesn't take much learnin' either. Not if you've any sense it doesn't. Me? I learned it very early on. It's why I'm sitting here enjoying my drink and you're there shittin' yourself."

He reached for his whisky again and then lit a cigarette. He pushed the pack and lighter across the table and nodded at Watson. The boy's hands were shaking as he took one, lit it and inhaled deeply. He looked across but Collins just sat looking back at him, expressionless, and the silence built again.

"She pregnant? Is that it?" he finally managed to say.

Collins leaned back and roared with laughter. "You still don't get this do you son?" He laughed again. "Pregnant? In a *week*? No. You're still alive aren't you? Christ, if she was pregnant and he knew you were the father you'd be dead. If he knew you'd even been there and she wasn't pregnant, you'd be dead. Pregnant?" He laughed again. "No, it's not that."

"You won't tell 'im we did, will you... you wouldn't do that to me..."

"I'll tell him what I bleedin' well like won't I?" Collins said, his voice suddenly hard. Watson clenched his buttocks so that he didn't foul himself.

"After all," Collins continued, "there's nobody else here, is there? And you sure as hell ain't gonna say anythin". Am I right?"

The boy nodded. "You're right."

Collins shook his head, still smiling. "This is none of your business, mind you but in the circumstances... no, he hasn't a clue what she's like where sex is concerned. Not a bleedin' clue. She's twenty, looking the way she does, dressing the way she does, and he still thinks she's a virgin. Still his little girl. Thinks 'cos he and his missus've never let her see them undressed and he always locks the bathroom door, she doesn't know what boys've got between their legs and what they want to do with it. Forgets she grew up with two brothers. He still sees her like she's takin' her first communion. And that's exactly how she is around him. So cute you wouldn't believe it. Talk about butter wouldn't melt."

"But that's not what she's..."

"Around him I said. He doesn't know what she's like when she's not there. Doesn't know who's screwin' her, doesn't know anybody's screwin' her. And I'll tell you this for nothing, I wouldn't want to be in the same country if he ever does find out." He stared past Watson for a moment or two as if picturing the scene. Then he shook his head slowly and took another drink

"The point is, she'd been knocked about a bit. And even a bit's, a bit too much. You'd given her a bit of a slapping son. A girl? That's breaking golden rule number one. And this is the man's only daughter for Christ's sake, and the youngest of his three. He lives for her. D'you understand what I'm saying here? If she told him to walk in front of a bus, he would. Now... you'd done it to one of his sons, been different. Different altogether. He wouldn't've been interested. Wouldn't even bothered mentioning it to me. He would've just told them to sort it out themselves. That's what boys are supposed to do. Sort it and not bother their father."

He shook his head again. "But this was his daughter. Jesus, son, it could've been *my* daughter. Vanishing with her after you left the club's bad enough. Screwin' her, well, at least that doesn't show... not for a few months anyway. But slappin' her? No. That was out of order, son. Well out of order."

"But you don't understand. She likes it," Watson pleaded, "She asked me to. Be rough, she said. It's what she wanted. She loves it!"

"Oh. Right," Collins said, shaking his head. "Well, that's okay then. I'll just tell him that will I? Don't worry about it, I'll say, it's her own fault. Your darlin' Lisa just happens to be kinky like that. Likes bein' knocked about a bit, it's what turns her on, Oh yeah. I can just hear my bleedin' self."

"But it's true! She..."

Collins's face closed down and his eyes hardened.

"Tell him your fucking self then," he said as Watson pressed his knees together to stop the shaking. Come with me now. I'll take you to him and you can tell him. Eh?"

Watson just shook his head.

"Thought not," Collins said. And I'm not going to tell 'im, that's for sure. I've got a stronger sense of survival than you seem to have. No, son, what you don't do with his daughter, or the daughter of anybody like him, what you don't do is buy them drinks all night, dance with them all night and then walk them out the place with every fucker watching. Including some well-known faces don't forget because it wasn't just stupid young boys like you who were there. What you also don't do is disappear with her for a couple of hours and then let her show up at home cryin', with marks on her face and bruises all over her arms and shoulders."

"But she..." Watson started to protest yet again.

"That is absolutely what you do not fucking do," Collins said, ignoring him. "Upsetting his missus as well. Don't do things by halves do you, son? Wife and daughter in the one night? That's too much even for a man like him. You weren't being fair to yourself, son. Kamikaze in fact. C'mon, son. You must've known it was her and what was likely to happen to you after."

"No, I didn't. Honest. Not at first. Not until one of my mates asked if I knew who it was I'd been dancin' with. I knew her name but that's common round here but he told me which Doyle. Then I knew."

"In the club? After you'd danced with her, but still in the club you mean?"

"Yeah," Watson mumbled, staring down at the floor between his feet. And almost in tears by now.

Collins shook his head. "Christ almighty! I was told you were just daft. Just a daft young boy. You're not, you're bleedin' mental. Somebody told you, in the club, and you still went back and danced with her again?"

"Yeah," Watson said. "Then the next day, my brother told me exactly who her old man is, told me exactly what he's like, what his reputation is an' that and I couldn't..."

"And you're still in London? I've got to hand it to you son. You've got some balls. They're where your brains should be mind, but you've certainly got a large pair."

"Where'm I gonna go, though?" He asked the question as if he expected Collins to give him the answer.

"Where?" Collins said, laughing again. "Anywhere, son. Anywhere a long way from London. He's big round here but got no real contacts anywhere else. And he wouldn't chase you anyway, not even for his precious daughter. Not onto somebody else's manor he wouldn't."

"Leave London? No, not now. I can't. I'm on the books at Spurs, an' I ain't givin' that up. I'll just have to stay here and take my chances. And anyway, it's not like it was. Nobody leaves London. Them that did only went as far as Essex."

"Not if they did what you've done. They wouldn't just go there. No bleedin' chance."

"No, no, I've got to think about my football. It's all I got. I've just cracked the reserves, played four times now..."

"Yeah, I know. One of my mates was tellin' me. Goes to all the games, reserves an' all, bleedin' well lives at White Hart Lane. He saw your game against Arsenal last week. Rated you highly. Said you'd promise, genuine promise. Why d'you think I'm bein' nice to you?" Collins asked as he finished his whisky.

"What..."

"It's one of the reasons I didn't really want to have to do this job. But then, I couldn't exactly say no, could I?"

"Job? What d'you mean job? I thought you said you were just asked to have a chat..."

"Come on, son," Collins said, shaking his head. "Where've you been livin' for the last nineteen years? You know the score as well as I do. And there's no nil-nils in this game. You know how it is. You give your Gran or your Mum some lip and your old man gives you a good smack. Do some young boy, and his brothers or his mates give you a doin' in return."

He put his hands out in front of him, palms up, as he spoke. "That's just the way it is. Fact of life. Right or wrong in other people's eyes doesn't come into it. You know that. They've never got past the Old Testament round here, son. Eye for an eye and all that. A minute ago you said you'd just have to stay here and take your chances. I couldn't believe my ears."

"But..."

"You talk about chances? I'm here, aren't I? Which means you only had two chances left. Slim and fuck all. And slim left town the minute I walked in this pub."

Watson tensed, put his hands on the edge of the table and looked round at the door.

"Give us a break son. Come on, how far d'you think you'd get? Stop dreamin'. You were stupid and you know it. You gave some out, to a girl as well, and you've got to get some back. Got to. It's that simple. It's why I'm here, it's what I do. And I'm good at it. You know that, you said it yourself."

"I know, I know. But I didn't really expect... I mean I knew somethin' might... but I didn't... I never... Oh Jesus." He was almost crying again.

"Wise up, son. And act your bleedin' age for gawd's sake. You know you can't walk away from it, so just get a bleedin' grip on yourself and take it, take what's comin' to you."

"But it's just not fair... you can't... I mean you just can't... I'm just a boy, for god's sake... not some hard case that's a threat to him... Gimme a break here, eh? Please, mister... You can't... you can't just top me in here, not..."

Collins burst out laughing again. "What? What did you just say? Top you?" Collins choked back his laughter as the boy started crying for real. "No, no, no. I don't murder children. You ain't gonna die here, son. No. He said to make it somethin' you'd never forget. Ever. Make it somethin' that'd always remind you of the need for good manners where women are concerned... you know? Somethin' worse than dyin' he said."

Watson knocked his pint and the stool flying as he scrambled to his feet. But he was much too slow. Collins was moving before he'd really thought about it. The boy didn't see the punch when it came, from somewhere beneath the table, he only knew he'd been hit because his jaw exploded, and he suddenly found himself lying face down on the floor. There was a roaring in his head and his vision was blurred. As he squirmed around, trying to work out where the rest of his body was, he felt Collins kneel on his back and grab both ankles in one hand.

He tried to struggle, tried to lift his hips and get to his knees, but an elbow in the back of his head and his face smashed into the floor was all he got in response. And the blade was so sharp he didn't actually feel any pain. Collins drew the old-fashioned, open razor hard and deep across both the boy's hamstrings. His screams came from the realisation of what was happening and what it meant to his hopes of playing at White Hart Lane, more than the sensation itself.

"Remember what I told you, son," Collins whispered. "Keep your dirty little hands to yourself in future. That's the message. I'd remember it if I were you. Else I'll be back to cut the bleedin' things clean off."

He straightened up, closed the razor into its ivory handle, slipped it into his overcoat pocket and walked casually through to the other room towards the door. Apart from Charlie Harris, who was nowhere in sight, nobody had moved, and nobody looked at him as the screams continued from the next room. Nobody except the barman.

"Ambulance job?" he asked.

"I'd say so," Collins said. "And that mop and bucket behind the bar there. Boy's had a bit of an accident."

Five

Collins left the pub and walked round the corner to his car. His new Jag. That he loved. He slid into the driver's seat but instead of taking in the leather and wood as he normally did, he just clenched the steering wheel in both hands and stared out of the window.

He thought about the mess he'd created in the pub. The job he'd just done was way out of the norm for him. Usually he was all business. Doling out punishment to guys who expected it when they fucked up. Who never complained because they understood it was just business. That was his reputation and people respected and feared him because of it. But this had been personal. Something the man couldn't trust his useless sons to sort out. Just a kid, for Christ's sake.

"Dave Collins," he whispered. "What the fuck have you just done?"

He continued to sit there, quietly staring into space until the sound of sirens, police and ambulance, jerked him out of it. He sighed, shook his head and turned the key. He shoved it into first and quickly pulled away.

He was much too preoccupied to see Charlie Harris slip out of a shop doorway on the other side of the street and step back into a telephone box.

WHAT'S A SIMPLE MAN TO DO

The house was a substantial, detached, four-bedroom property, with huge mature gardens, set in a quiet, leafy road in suburban Wimbledon. Dinner was over, having been served at precisely six-thirty, as it was every night of the week except Sunday, when dinner became lunch, dished up at twelve-thirty. Such was the unvarying mealtime-driven timetable. The elderly husband and his much younger wife were relaxing in the garden lounge, the dishes, cutlery and glasses having been removed and carefully arranged in the dishwasher. By the husband, of course, since she could never do it his satisfaction. Of course.

It was late August, still warm, and the French doors leading to the patio and the garden were wide open. Had it not been for the mobile phones on the side tables and the wide-screen plasma TV above the fireplace where the mirror used to hang, it could have been a scene from the 1930s. A scene that was only disturbed only by the sounds coming from upstairs. The bathroom door and a bedroom door slamming in quick succession. With a short burst of loud music as one opened and closed. The father raised his eyebrows and shook his head.

"Does that blessed girl have to make quite so much damn noise?"

"Oh, I quite like a bit of noise at times, Edwin," his wife said. "Makes it feel as if the house is alive."

He ignored that. Just grunted. "Not that kind of banging and slamming, though. And that caterwauling she has the nerve to call music." He shook his head in irritation. "I shall have a word with her when she comes down."

"Now Edwin," his wife said, "Don't start. Leave the girl alone. I won't have you ruining her evening before she's even left the house."

He glared at her across the room. His book forgotten; he was sitting in his favourite armchair - the one nobody else dares to sit in. His wife was on the sofa opposite engrossed in a gardening programme on her iPad. He grunted again at the sound of their daughter's clumping footsteps as she trotted noisily downstairs. She walked into the lounge and stopped when she saw the expression on his face. And took in her mother's quick shake of the head.

"Hello you two. Discussing all my good points, are we?" she asked with a giggle. Feeling the nice buzz from the two large vodkas she'd had in her bedroom.

Her father looked her up and down and sighed heavily.

The daughter laughed and did a balletic twirl, arms out wide. She knows that the t-shirt bearing the words, 'A woman's place is exactly where she wants it to be', the artfully ripped black leggings underneath the short, tight, black skirt, and her heavy brown boots will never meet with his approval.

Nor will her piercings, although three in each ear with a discreet diamond in her left nostril is positively understated these days. Good job he never sees me naked, she thought. Lord alone knows what he would make of the piercings in my belly button. And his reaction if he ever saw the three tattoos didn't bear thinking about.

"You're disappointing me, Pa," she said. I was expecting to hear, "you're never going out dressed like that, young lady, are you?"

Her mother smiled and tapped the screen to pause her programme. Don't need any electronic entertainment now the cabaret has started, she thought.

"Well, you are quite wrong," he said. "I was about to say I hope you don't have to go through any metal detectors this evening because you'd never make it."

Her mother smiled again, and the daughter laughed.

"Ah, the old ones really aren't the best, Pa. Dad jokes just don't do it anymore. You need to get yourself a new script writer."

Her father just stared. "Glad I amuse you, young lady," he said.

"But you wouldn't if you didn't say such ridiculous things," she said, laughing again. "You're an absolute hoot when you get going."

"I did warn you Edwin," his wife said, laughing along with her daughter.

"Will somebody rescue me from this monstrous regimen of women," he said.

"From flippant humour to classical allusion. Nice one, Pa. Although I seriously doubt that the mere two of us qualify either as a regimen, or monstrous," his daughter said. She walked across the room and checked her make up one last time in the mirror over the fireplace.

"Perhaps not," he replied, "but it's the impact of the two of you, your total lack of respect, that's what's monstrous."

She turned to face him. "All in all, I'd have thought you've done pretty bloody well from our impact. You never cook, clean, decorate, do the ironing, or shopping. The only thing you do in the garden is mow the lawns. And that's just because you have that super, sit-on machine that you love so much. I bet you imagine you're mowing the wicket at Lords, or the Centre Court at Wimbledon as you're whizzing around."

"Lizzie, please don't rise to his bait," her mother said. "You know what he's like."

"How can I resist, though mum, when he feeds me such good material." She turned to face her father again. "Mum does everything while I pitch in and help with it all. You know, all the stuff that would mean you having to get your hands dirty. Your little two-women regimen pretty much do everything for you, Pa."

"You're forgetting that I pay all the bills young lady."

"Ah, the fascism of the elderly, monied male of the species. What is that exactly, Pa? Our wages? Servant's payments, perhaps? Do we have to walk backwards from the room, bowing and tugging our forelocks in humble gratitude? Partnerships are built on more than servitude and monetary recompense, father dear."

Her father glared at her as his fingers beat a tattoo on the arm of the chair. "Be that as it may and you might well mock, but paying all the bills – including, may I remind you, your extremely expensive education – is not inconsequential."

Lizzie laughed. "Honestly, the way you talk, at times, Pa."

"I use language precisely and while I quite understand that is not the custom these days, I offer no apology for using words that convey a precise meaning."

"You do indeed," Lizzie said. "Noel Coward and his velvet jacket would have been proud of you, Pa."

Her mother stifled a laugh and indicated with her head that Lizzie should leave. As she turned towards the door her father called out to her. "So where are you off to tonight young lady?"

"Lizzie, Pa, that's my name. Lizzie. Remember? After all you did give it to me. Or did you leave that to Mum as well?"

"You were christened Elizabeth, young lady, as well you know. I simply do not understand why you young people have to abbreviate everything."

"Not quite everything, Pa. I mean, I never call you Ed or Eddie, do I?" She winked at her mother who somehow managed to keep a straight face.

"As for where I'm going, the simple answer is out! And Mel's waiting for me in the car, so I'd best be off."

"I didn't hear the car," her father said.

"That's because she's parked out on the road," Lizzie said. "After the way you spoke to her the last time she was here, she refuses to come in ever again."

"That's ridiculous. I merely engaged the girl in conversation. I simply asked her some pertinent questions, that's all."

His wife snorted. "Simply asked her some pertinent questions? No Edwin, you did not. You were overbearing, rude, and aggressive. And it's not girl either. She's a grown woman of thirty-four for goodness' sake and you spoke to her as though she were a young child – and not a very bright one at that. I don't blame Mel at all for waiting out on the road. I'd do the same."

"I was merely enquiring as to her intentions regarding Elizabeth, that was all."

"What nonsense, Edwin," his wife said. "I know it pains you dear but we're not living in Victorian times. Or would you be happier in the Edwardian period? Because that sort of questioning is quite inappropriate these days. Especially when same sex relationships are involved."

"Yes," Lizzie said. "Because if I'd brought a young man home you wouldn't have questioned his sexuality, now would you?"

"Obviously not because there would have been no need. You're hardly likely to get involved with a gay boy, are you?"

Lizzie and her mother both laughed and shook their heads.

"Pa, you're impossible, you know that? I have a lot of gay friends, but I wouldn't be able to socialise with them ever again if I brought them here and introduced them to you," Lizzie said. "Anyway, enough of all this, I'm off. Night both and don't wait up."

Her mother smiled again and offered her cheek for a kiss. Lizzie gave her a quick peck and walked out of the room. "Laters," she called as they heard the front door open and close.

Lizzie walked down the drive to the gate and spotted Mel's Mini parked a few yards away. As she approached, she saw Mel raise her eyebrows and lift her hands, palms up, in the universal sign of, 'where the hell have you been?'.

Oh, god, Lizzie thought. Here we go again. A little bit of fun with my father to get the evening off to a nice start and now this. I'm supposed to be having a love affair, not being a partner in a toxic marriage. I am getting so, so tired of this. She slid into the car and fastened her seat belt.

"Well?" Mel said.

"Well, what?"

"What took you so long? I've been sitting here for almost fifteen minutes." Without waiting for a reply, Mel thumped the car into gear and drove off.

"Nothing to say for yourself?" she asked a few minutes later.

"Sorry, yes. I love the seat belt in this little car. The way it crosses over my chest makes me look as if I've got a proper pair of tits."

"Don't be flip, Lizzie, it really doesn't become you. And don't try to change the subject. What happened?"

Lizzie sighed. "Nothing *happened*, Mel. Dad just decided he wanted a discussion about what I was wearing and where I was going. So me and Mum had some fun with him. Hasn't lasted long though."

"I don't know how you stand it, Lizzie," Mel said, ignoring or completely missing Lizzie's little barb. "Doesn't he realise you're a grown woman of twenty-six, not some silly sixteen-year-old?"

Oh, not again, Lizzie thought. How many times are we going to have this bloody discussion.

"Of course he does. It's just his way, Mel. And I stand it because I know he loves me deeply, cares about me, and would do anything for me. I can forgive him almost anything because of that. And I love him."

"How can you say he loves and cares for you when he doesn't accept and respect you for the person you are?" Lizzie asked, an edge to her voice now.

"But he does. You don't understand, Mel. Don't want to, I think. He just has very old-fashioned ideas about what families should be. Home, kids… and especially daughters."

"Old fashioned? From what you tell me, he's positively prehistoric. Stupidly so."

"No, he's not stupid at all, Mel. Far from it. You have to remember he was fifty-two when I was born which makes him a seventy-eight-year-old man. And one who comes from a completely different era. A completely different world. And he was a confirmed bachelor 'til he met mum, don't forget. A lot of his friends and colleagues wondered if he was gay."

"That's irrelevant. Your mother's not like that at all." And what my mum is like compared to my dad is equally irrelevant Lizzie thought. But let's deal with this.

"Yes, that maybe so, but she's twenty-five years younger than him. Which makes a huge difference. The point I'm trying to make is that he simply hasn't quite come to terms with the modern world. His view of life is set firmly in the 1950s when children did as they were told - or else - and they had to meet their parents' expectations. When women stayed at home and busied themselves with the house, children and taking care of the husband. When 'good' women didn't smoke in public and didn't go into pubs on their own. And when Gays and Lesbians were rumoured to exist but were seldom seen and never heard."

Mel seemed to ignore all that and half turned as she was driving. "But if he's intelligent as you say, how can he not be aware that the world has changed?"

"Oh, for god's sake. Of course he's aware. He knows, he just doesn't see why he should have to understand or accept it. He's long retired and insulated from what's happening out in the world today - I'm the only connection, really – and he doesn't accept that it has anything to do with him. He has no reference points. He's mildly irritating at times, sure, which of us isn't? But he's not a bad man at all, Mel, surely you can understand that."

Mel shook her head and turned again in her seat. "You have got to get out of there, Lizzie. Living with him is preventing you from realising your full potential. He's stunting your growth."

Lizzie leaned back and closed her eyes, thinking it would be best just to let this go. Keep quiet, let it run its course and then enjoy the rest of the evening. But quickly thought no, the evening is ruined already, there's no recovering it, and I am not putting up with this nonsense again.

"Wait a second, Mel. You're telling me? Who and what I am, who I should be and what I should do with my life? How I should regard my father and what our relationship should be? I don't believe this. We've been here before and you don't seem to hear me when I explain it to you. Who said you were the arbiter of the person I should be? Who made you the authority on my life? Do I not have any say in that? I seem to remember you were the one who said that only partnerships of equals could flourish. Yet here you are telling me what I should and shouldn't do. What I can and can't be? Seriously? Where's the respect for my intelligence and judgement? Where's the equality in that? Please tell me because I'm more than curious."

Mel laughed. "Wow! That was quite the little rant there, Lizzie. But I have to explain it to you because sometimes we simply can't see what's happening to ourselves and we need someone to explain it."

"But I've just told you, Mel. Explained it to you in some detail. So of course I see it. Don't you get that? Accept that?"

Mel smiled and placed her hand on Lizzie's thigh. "I just think you've entered 'dutiful daughter' phase - if indeed you ever escaped it. I had such high hopes for you Lizzie, but you really are beginning to disappoint me."

"Oh I am, am I?" she said, yanking Mel's arm away. "Stop the car. Now! Pull into that bus stop! Just do it!"

Mel braked, pulled in left and stopped. She turned to look at Lizzie.

"I disappoint you, Mel? Oh really? You arrogant, patronising cow. You sounded just like my dad but without any of the excuses he has. Do you know, I used to hang on your every word, yearn for your approval. But now? I'm finding I no longer care about your judgements. I've no interest in what you think about me. I know exactly what my relationship is with my father, thank you very much. I know why it is, why I'm okay with it and I don't need to listen to you delivering your pathetic, pseudo-feminist judgements about it".

Mel shook her head. Smirk at me and I'll slap you, Lizzie thought.

"But I think you do," Mel said. Because I can see you're losing your perspective. You simply can't become truly whole if you're still in father-fixation mode, Lizzie. One prevents the other and I'm surprised you can't see that."

Lizzie unbuckled her seat belt. "You know, I didn't think you could be any more patronising, but you've just excelled yourself. I know you're eight years older than me, Mel, a lot more experienced, but I don't need a teacher, tutor, or a mentor. I refuse to be your little personal project any longer, so you just take your facile analysis, your social bloody grooming and shove it. Go work it out on somebody else."

"Ah, is this your true self is coming out now Lizzie. Such undeveloped male aggression."

"D'you know what, Mel, just fuck off. Fuck off and stay fucked off. Is that male enough for you? Or are we women not supposed to use language like that?"

Mel laughed. "What? Is that you finishing it? Finishing us? Is this the end?"

There was a silence while Lizzie took a deep breath and collected herself.

"That's a very good question. And yes. Yes, I think I am. No, I know I am. It's been fun and the sex was pretty good - at least in the early days it was, spectacular even - but I've already got a mother, thank you. And one who doesn't preach to me the way you do, telling me what I should be doing and thinking all the time. I don't need another, inferior, one, thank you."

"It's sad in a way, but you really have turned out to be a disappointment to me, Lizzie, you know that?"

"Really? Well, if I didn't before, I do now. And you know what? I don't give a shit. So why don't you just... just fuck off, Mel."

Lizzie got out of the car and slammed the door. She took out her mobile and thumbed in a number as she watched Mel drive away. It was answered almost immediately.

"Hi Robyn, it's me. Are you by any chance still free tonight? And does your offer still stand?"

"Hey babe! Nice surprise. Yes, I am, and yeah, 'course it does. But I thought you were going out with the old crone tonight," she said, laughter in her voice.

"Stop it you. I've had enough this evening already. And just so you know, tonight was the last one. Ever."

"Really? Thank god for that," Robyn said. "But what happened? Do tell."

"I'll tell all later," Lizzie said. "So where do you want to meet?"

"Nowhere. Just come round here," Robyn said. "I've just made the pizza dough in my clever little machine. I've got red wine, Prosecco, Tequila, and... chocolate! And I've got a brand-new toy if you feel like being a bit naughty later on."

"If I have enough of all that booze you've got, I can be as naughty as you want... in fact, I need to celebrate, so I'm up for being very naughty indeed."

"How much is enough?"

"Oh, you'll know, Robyn. You'll know. See you in ten."

"I'll stick the pizza in now and open the red. See ya."

Lizzie ended the call and then phoned for an Uber. Feeling lighter and happier than she had in months.

Three

"The problem is, she's got a mind of her own that one. Likes the sound of her own voice too much."

"Well, that's how we raised her Edwin, isn't it? We always encouraged her to think things through for herself and not live on second-hand opinions all the time. We can hardly complain if she learned well. All in all, I think we were pretty successful. Yes, we didn't do a bad job at all I'd say."

"Successful? Are you being serious?"

"Perfectly, Edwin. Never more so."

"But just look at her. My only daughter. A lesbian! And she's a bloody socialist!"

His wife laughed and shook her head. "Oh grade them do you, Edwin dear? Award degrees of failure? I see. So, tell me. Which is worse in your book, her being a socialist, a lesbian, or the fact that she's an intelligent, educated, strong-minded young woman who is confident, articulate and forthright? Or is it all three? What are you saying exactly?"

"Don't you go putting words in my mouth, woman."

"Well that's where they fell from, Edwin. I just picked them up, put them all together and fed them back to you."

"Yes, very droll my dear. But levity won't deviate me. It's simply that she's been such a disappointment to me in some ways."

His wife shook her head and sighed. "She's a disappointment, Edwin? I don't understand you sometimes. Really I don't. She got into Cambridge, graduated with first class honours, has a good job and as soon as she has the deposit, she'll buy her own place. Won't accept us funding her, even with a loan. I wouldn't call that disappointing. Compare her to some of the children of our friends. No university, dead end jobs, some with drug problems even. If you're having difficulty with Lizzie, just think how much worse it would be trying to come to terms with them."

"Well, yes, Cambridge I suppose…"

"You suppose? What*ever* do you mean by that?"

"What I meant was it might well have been Cambridge, but it was only Newnham College after all. A women's college. No doubt that's where she learned to become a lesbian…"

"Edwin! For god's sake! Where "*she learned to become a lesbian*". Will you listen to yourself? Lizzie's right, you really are insufferable at times."

"And a first in what was it, Psychology? He said, interrupting her. "Dear God, what possible good is that to anyone? Neither use to man nor beast. She'll never earn decent money working with… how does she describe them again… differently-abled children?" Whatever that is supposed to mean."

His wife closed her iPad, put her glasses on the side table, walked across and sat on the arm of his chair. "I've said it before and I'll say it again, Edwin. Working all those years in a Merchant Bank where your Christmas bonus alone was ten times what the average man was earning, has given you a completely distorted view of work and money. I'm not denying it's very nice to have absolutely no money worries at all but it's not the only thing in life - possibly not even the most important. She is a highly qualified, professional young woman and so long as she isn't stupid, which she isn't and won't be, she'll be absolutely fine. Trust me on that."

Edwin nodded an acknowledgement and then there was a lengthy silence. Finally, he looked up at her and spoke.

"The difficulty I have is that I had hoped for a white wedding… saw myself walking her down the aisle. Giving my daughter away. Properly. Afterwards with her living not too far away. A good marriage to a suitable chap with prospects, then grandchildren while I'm still alive. You know, what most parents hope for."

She noticed his eyes had become moist, so she put her hand on his arm and gently squeezed. "But you can't create some ideal fantasy for yourself and expect Lizzie to live her life in a way that perfectly matches it. Life simply doesn't work that way, Edwin. So I'm sorry Lizzie doesn't meet all your expectations. But they're yours, not hers, dear, and trying constantly to impose them on her is totally unreasonable. Unacceptable in fact."

"I realise that, but…"

"No, let me finish. You'll just have to learn to love and respect her for the impressive young woman she is as well as respecting the decisions she makes in her life. If you can do that then you will enjoy her and what she becomes. If you don't then you run the serious risk of losing her. And knowing you as I do, you would find that unbearable."

"I suppose you're right," Edwin said with a sigh. "But you'll have to help me to get there, you do realise that don't you?"

"Of course, Edwin, and we shall, you know. We shall. Together."

But I'm not banking on it, she thought as she kissed his forehead and went off to have her bath, leaving him to his own thoughts and fractured hopes and dreams.

THE PENULTIMATE SONG

He was lost in the music. Absorbing it into his brain rather than actively listening. While he reflected on his life. Introspection, which invariably tends to centre on the negatives, was something his wife had often warned him against. People actually like you for who you are, she'd said. Because you're a good man, Matthew, a nice man. You should learn to accept that, and be kinder to yourself, she'd told him. He had to ask her to remind him how that worked again. She just smiled and shook her head.

But she was right in that, as she was with most things. Especially where people and feelings were concerned. But he found it hard to accept when he examined his behaviour with those people who were not his clients. He was scrupulously polite, and fair, with them and so gained their respect, if not their friendship. But was that enough? He somehow doubted it when he considered how he treated other people. Especially those who crossed his lines where his view of acceptable human behaviour was concerned.

His train of thought was broken when he felt the earphones being slowly eased out. Irritated, he opened his eyes but quickly relaxed when he saw the woman smiling at him. And her smile had always lifted him since the day he'd first seen it. He smiled back at her and then raised his eyebrows in silent question.

"Sorry," she said, resting her hand lightly on his shoulder. "But you didn't hear me speak. You were miles away. I thought you were asleep before I saw the 'phones. What's that you're listening to?"

"A song about motorbikes," he told her. "Written by an Englishman and sung by a Scot. A song about a motorbike called a Vincent Black Lightning."

"And what's that when it's at home?" she asked. "I've never heard of it."

"I'd be surprised if a young woman your age did know about it. A masterpiece, it was. Hand built by true artisans. Best quality engineering and workmanship. The most lusted after bike of its day. My uncle had one for racing and had its sister bike, the Black Shadow for socialising because it had a pillion seat for girls to ride on... sorry, way before your time, I'm just wittering on here," he said.

She smiled. "No, it's interesting... and something I can work into the conversation to impress the men."

"Huh, I shouldn't have thought anybody as beautiful as you would need to do anything to impress them except just be."

"You'd be surprised, some of the arseholes I meet - 'scuse my French."

"But who'd want to impress arseholes anyway?"

She laughed. "You know, you're absolutely right. But I seem to have to. Arseholes are pretty much all I ever seem to meet these days. And a good man is hard to find, isn't that what they say?'

"Thought it was 'a hard man is good to find'. Isn't that how they put it?" he said with a grin. She laughed again.

"That's one of the problems of being beautiful you know," he said.

"What is?"

"The sort of men who ask you out will be mainly interested in your looks. Having a beautiful woman on their arm to impress their friends. They're not really interested in you as a person, just as a sort of human ornament. Arseholes, like you said. But the decent men, the more shy, less confident, less good-looking ones, they wouldn't dare ask you out in case you said no. In fact, inside their heads, they'd be bloody sure you'd say no."

She frowned and nodded. "I think you might be right."

"I know I am. Because I was one of the non-arseholes and it didn't do me much good 'til I met my wife. Although to be truthful, she made all the running. I was astonished."

"Was she beautiful, then? Is that what you're saying?"

"They say that beauty is in the eye of the beholder, don't they? Well in my eyes, she was the most beautiful woman I'd ever seen. And I thought that 'til the day she went and died on me. Broke a promise she did. We always said I would go first. But if I'm honest," he said, "she wasn't beautiful the way you are."

The young woman blushed.

"More beautiful than the most beautiful woman you'd ever seen?" she said. "I don't think anybody's ever paid me a bigger compliment. Okay then, since you're my captive beauty expert, what can I do about it - if anything?"

"Encourage the others. Let them know you're interested. You don't have to be brazen, just be kind with the shy ones when it's needed. Kindness works every time."

There was a brief silence as she thought about what he'd said. "That song really affected you," she said. "Made you all philosophical."

"The song always surprises me, is what it is," he said. "Because it makes me feel fifteen again. Made me fifteen again for almost five minutes."

She shook her head and again frowned the question.

"No, no, it's a good thing. Really. I just loved being fifteen. My favourite age. I used to tell my wife it was the main reason I was so attracted to her in my thirties. She made me feel fifteen again. You know, all the things I wanted to say to her were clear in my head but my throat got so tight, my tongue so thick and my heart pounded so much I couldn't get them out."

He grinned, remembering the first time he'd dared ask her out. A grown man shaking, only alcohol giving him the courage.

"She'd let me know through a mutual friend that she was interested but I was just so terrified that, even so, she'd say no. Like the men who want to ask you out but daren't. Or worse, she'd just laugh at me. Being as worried about a woman's reaction then, as I was at parties when I was fifteen, was a strange but wonderful feeling. Do you remember ever feeling like that?" he asked her.

She just smiled and shook her head.

"It was half your brain saying, "go on, ask, say it, the worst they can do is say no." And the other half saying, "but if I do and they say no, I couldn't bear it, I'll fucking die."

That was not something she had ever experienced, the young woman told him.

"No? No, maybe not. You were probably always one of those beautiful girls who could just wait patiently until all us hopeless boys finally managed to get some words out, and then take your pick of one of the best looking." He studied her carefully. "Yes... looking at you and thinking about it, you probably were. I'd never have been able to pluck up the courage to ask you to dance."

"I would have if you'd been around to ask me", she said. "I still would, actually."

"Huh. Bloody shame my dancing days are over, in that case. But thank you for the compliment. You know, in my mind I'm not actually the man who's lying here. I'm the younger, fitter me, with a real life. A dancer. The dancer I was back then. But reality always kicks in and I have to accept that this is all there is, all there ever will be now. There'll be no more dancing for me."

"And there was me thinking I knew you," she said. "But you can still surprise me after all this time. And it's not as bad as you think, you know. Life never is."

"Oh yes, full of surprises, me. Except for optimism. I won't surprise you with anything like that. Because the more I look back on my life, the more incomplete I feel - less of a man, I'd say. Though, in truth, I was never much of a man. In my sixty-eight years I have left barely a scratch on anyone's consciousness except my wife and children. And even then only momentarily. They tolerated me for what I was - part lover, part protector, part supplier, part humourist, and part, especially latterly, figure of fun."

Then he was lost again. She sat, waiting patiently because she liked this quietly spoken man who flirted with her in way that caused her no offence. Suddenly his eyes opened, and he began talking to her again. Partly to her, but mostly to himself, she thought.

He told her that something broke when his wife died. He found himself withdrawing into his own world and his children drifted away from him. It wasn't sudden, he said, not caused by a single event, he just gradually became aware that a distance had grown between them. And since he had no idea what the causes were, he didn't know how to lessen it.

"Eventually I found I didn't care, hadn't the energy or will to care, and became reconciled to the situation. And here we are."

Another silence grew then, and she didn't know how to reply to those revelations so she simply said, "But the motorbikes... you were going to tell me about them?"

He looked at her in surprise. "Are you sure you want to hear all this?"

"Yes, of course. Even if it's a subject I've never been particularly interested in, I love hearing people talk about something they're passionate about. And I already know you're a wonderful story-teller."

"Okay," he said, surprise registering in his voice. And pleasure. "Well, the motorbikes. Never had one myself but I'd grown up surrounded by them. Three of my uncles owned them and the one who lived nearest, Reuben – they had names like that in the fifties - used to take me for rides in his sidecar. Do you remember sidecars? Are you old enough?"

She smiled and shook her head again.

"They were everywhere in the days when people couldn't afford family cars," he said. "You could take the wife and three kids if you had a decent sidecar. Reuben had a bike called an Ariel Square Four and he had a huge Swallow sidecar to go with it. The Ariel was massive, a four-cylinder 1,000cc 'bike built purely for pulling sidecars. All bottom end power and no top speed. But a great sensation of noise and movement when you're a little kid riding six inches away from all that heat and noise."

"You didn't ride on the back of the 'bike then?" she asked.

"Good god no! Not back then. Too young. For grown-ups only. Had to ride in the sidecar 'til I turned eleven. Great age, eleven, as well. First pair of long trousers and allowed to ride on the back of a motorbike. How good was that?"

He closed his eyes again and fell silent. After a minute or so she gently touched his shoulder.

"Reuben," she said, "You were telling me about Reuben."

"Sorry, yes. It's like a bad Billy Connolly story, going all around the houses before coming back to the point. Anyway. Reuben. Yes. He always wore an ankle-length khaki coat with straps which fastened around his calves to stop it flapping about in the wind. I always think of him when I see these Westerns with all the bad guys riding around in those wonderful long duster coats. He would've made a great member of the Dalton Gang, Reuben."

She laughed. "The Dalton gang? Now you've gone to another subject that I know nothing about. But we'll leave that for another time."

"Reuben was the first man I ever saw who smoked his pipe upside down on a motorbike. With a little perforated, hinged, silver lid to stop the tobacco falling out. Just so he could smoke his pipe while riding the 'bike without the sparks blowing into his face."

"You're pulling my leg now aren't you?" she asked, laughing again.

"No! Honestly, I'm not. It was quite common back with the old guys back in the day. Even better, he had brown, leather, lace-up boots that almost reached his knees. Always highly polished, of course. I always thought of him as this great, tall figure, wreathed in the smells of tobacco, 'bikes and leather. Then I met him again a few years ago at a family funeral. And he was shorter than me! Just goes to prove my theory that boyhood heroes, like rock stars, should die young and save us all that disillusionment."

She laughed. "A bit extreme I'd say but I understand what you mean. Certain people belong to a particular time and they shouldn't exist beyond it."

"Yes! Exactly. You get it. Not that many people do. Anyway, where was I. Ah yes, so I loved 'bikes and when I was fifteen, my older brother had two mates who were heavily into them. Geordie Wilson and Andy Niven. And I loved being round them. Not just for the bikes of course, being around the older boys was enough. Had my first taste of beer from them... and my first cigarette. I was fourteen. Couldn't say no when one of the big lads offered you. But I wished I hadn't. Not now I bloody don't"

"You don't now though, do you? Smoke I mean."

"No. I got some sense in my fifties and gave up. But if it hadn't been the fags it would have been something else. It's just what happened back then."

"But he didn't mind? You hanging around him and his friends?"

"Who? My brother you mean? My brother? Our kid?"

"Our kid? But I thought he was older."

"He was. Sorry I keep forgetting you're not from Newcastle, are you?"

She smiled. "No, not quite. Surrey's a long way away."

"Different country," he said. "So no, you wouldn't understand. Up here "our kid" doesn't mean younger, it's used about siblings of all ages. And as a greeting between close friends. But no, he didn't mind me hanging around. So long as I didn't show him up, he was fine."

"And did you?"

"Never. I was a little prick then, but not a stupid little prick, so I behaved myself, never embarrassed him. And that was the first time I realised he was one of life's good guys. And he never changed. Always protected me, looked after me, put me first even when his mates were involved."

"Sounds a rare man for back then."

"Oh he was. Then and always." He drifted for a while. She watched him, patiently waiting for him to come back from his reverie.

"His mates," she said. "You were telling me about them."

"Yes, I was… sorry, yes, being around them was good but being near their girlfriends, the older girls, was even better. Well, girls with lipstick, mascara, and breasts, with bras as pointed as their shoes. When fourteen and fifteen-year-old girls back then were still wearing white socks, sandals and trainer bras that flattened and hid it all from you."

"Wonderful," she said. "But I'm too young to remember all that."

"Don't keep reminding me," he said. "But if I kept quiet enough for long enough, they eventually forgot I was four or five years younger - or that I was even there at all - and carried on talking about the sorts of things they always talked about. All the sorts of things your mother prayed you never heard talked about. Especially by women. Because they were bad girls. Liked doing bad things. Naughty things. And I loved them for it. No surprise I've never to this day liked good girls. No fun in them at all. None."

She took his hand then and sat down beside him.

"Niven was an arrogant bastard - not without reason though since he had a 1962 Triumph Bonneville. Yes, yes," he said when she shook her head, "I know, but trust me it was the 'bike back then. The lads who rode Nortons would argue it, but the Bonneville was the one. Niven was also an arrogant bastard who hated little brothers more than he hated blokes who rode mopeds - but not as much as the Mods who rode scooters. They were definitely top of his hate list."

He shook his head and smiled.

"Geordie Wilson though, well, he was just different. One of those rare late teenagers who just seemed to love kids and never minded having them around. He had two younger brothers and a little sister and a mum and dad who never seemed to be there much, so maybe that had something to do with it."

"He used to take me for rides on his 'bike. On it. Not in some old boy's sidecar. Sorry, Reuben. Because he had another of the all-time classics - not that we realised it then, of course. A beautiful BSA Gold Star, 500cc single cylinder. One cylinder the size of a bucket. All dark green, black and chrome. A genuine road racing 'bike."

"I'll have to Google these when I've a moment," she said. "See the pictures along with the images you're giving me."

"Yes, do that. You'll see I'm not exaggerating. Anyway, I used to walk half a mile from my house, and he'd pick me up. With my old man I had to get that far away. If he'd seen me… 'What? Having fun? And dangerous fun at that? Have a fucking fist in the head, that'll teach you."

She laughed then.

"What?" he asked, irritation rising again.

"Just the way you describe it. You paint such a picture. He can't have been that bad."

"You want to bet? He was much worse than bad. Communication to him was issuing instructions, orders, then reinforcing the message with his fists if you didn't do things exactly as he wanted them done, when he wanted them done. Never mind if you'd done them right, if it wasn't how he wanted it, you were in trouble. He was a fucking psychopath."

She laughed again. "Sorry," she said, "it's just I've never heard you swear before – oh the occasional "bugger" and "damn", but never the "f" word."

His father and grandfather had both been coal miners, he told her and swearing was simply part of the vocabulary when only men were present. But never in front of the women. 'Bloody' and 'damn' were the strongest words he'd ever heard in mixed company. But as he grew older, he realised how sexist that was, especially when her heard women swearing. So he gradually relaxed into to swearing when he felt it necessary. Unless it was in front of much older women, his grandmother's generation for example who would genuinely find it offensive.

"So it's me who should apologise. I don't know you all that well and I'd hate to offend you," he said.

Genuinely. He loved this woman.

"No, no, it's fine. My father was a mechanical engineer. In a factory. Industrial language was the norm in our house, except, as you said, when my mum wasn't around. It was just because it's the first time I've heard you do it. Go on, tell me about your rides."

"Well, I'd climb aboard, no helmet, you could do that in those days, hands casually on your thighs or holding the back of the seat going fast round corners. Absolutely no hanging on to the rider. Only poofs – okay, gays," he said when she gave him a look. "It's just that's what we called them back then. Only gays and girls hung on to the rider."

"The girls did it of course whether they needed to or not," he said with a grin. "Clutching your fella round the waist sent a message to the other girls more than simply hanging on ever did. So, we'd go carefully down through Bell's Close, along the Scotswood Road over Scotswood Bridge and, never having broken the speed limit so the coppers had no reason to pull you over, on we went, down to Bikers' heaven."

"Bikers' heaven," she said. "What on earth was that?"

"The old Team Valley trading estate. Your typical post-war development built on the flood plain that was left when the river diverted centuries before. A long, flat, flood plain. With the estate made up of light industrial factories and storage units either side of a long concrete road. A long, straight, concrete road, over a mile long, with a roundabout at the top end. A place where in the evening and on Sundays there was no traffic, no speed limit and no coppers. It was perfect."

"Perfect for what? I don't get it."

"Never ridden on a motorbike then?"

"Goodness no. Never had a boyfriend who was into them. Only cars. Guess you'd say I've never lived."

"No, I'd never say that. But you've certainly missed something for sure."

He fell silent again and she just held his hand and waited. She only spoke when his eyes opened.

"The trading estate? What was it you were you saying?"

"Oh yes, where was I again? Oh yes, me and Geordie Wilson. Well… Geordie would cruise up to the roundabout and straighten up. Then a quick, hard, dip of the wrist and my eyeballs would be spread against the back of my brain and my arse would be flying off the back mudguard. I hung on then. Oh yes. But the sides of the seat. Never to him. Because even in the instant panic you didn't ever forget the basic rules. I did the ton for the first time when I was fifteen on that Trading Estate."

"The ton?" she asked.

"Hundred miles an hour - a ton", he explained. "The holy grail back then. I lost my virginity that year as well, but I was more proud of the fact that I'd done over a hundred miles an hour on the back of Geordie Wilson's Goldie. Crouched forward, head over his shoulder, wind-tears streaming back to my ears."

"It stopped when I was sixteen, though. Not because of me, but because of the consequences of the big lads playing chicken."

"Chicken?" she asked, squeezing his hand again, "what do you mean?"

"What they had to do," he said, "they had to ride up behind something big, big enough to completely block their view of oncoming traffic. A lorry or, better, a double-decker bus. Right up behind it at twice the speed or more than it was doing. Then, just before they piled into the back of it, they'd suddenly pull out, cross the white line, and accelerate like mad. Not surprisingly, quite a few died. Andy Niven was one of the lucky ones. Ended up as the sandwich filling between a yellow corporation bus and a coal lorry. Hobbled about on a leg and bit thereafter."

"But Geordie, well... he went out better than Eddie Cochran... old Rock 'n' Roll singer, don't worry about it. Spanking it up the A1, pulled out from behind a huge lorry, smack into the front of an eight-wheeler loaded with twenty tons of flour. At a terminal velocity of one hundred and twenty miles an hour. The driver and his mate were unharmed, but Geordie ended up in more pieces than his bike. And in more places. They were still finding bits of him days afterwards. Most of the lads lost heart after that and stopped doing it."

"I'm not surprised," she said.

"At the same time, I used to go to the Midlands in the school holidays to stay with my uncle Norman, another of my boyhood heroes. He also had motorbikes. Two of them. He had a car as well, a Wolseley, but that was only to keep the rain off my aunt. He had a 1936, JAP-engined, OK Supreme and, best of all, a 1950s hand-built Vincent Black Shadow, one of the all-time, classic 'bikes."

"He used to take me to watch Grand Prix racing at Oulton Park, where I not only got Giacomo Agostini's autograph, but also touched Mike Hailwood. Actually touched him! Gods, they were, gods. Not like those nancy-boy Premiership footballers you've got today. Real men."

"Anyway, he took me to scrambling races as well - Moto-cross they call it these days - all over Notts and Derbyshire. He'd raced as a young man, been a member of the Vincent works team. And his friends had been racers as well. They were great days. Which, sorry, is a very long-winded way to explain why a song about a classic Vincent Black Lightning, 1952, reaches me so much."

She smiled and squeezed his hand yet again. She liked the little squeeze she got in response each time.

"No. There's really no need to apologise. At all. You really should listen to music more," she said, "I've never heard you talk so much. And I only came in to tell you that your daughter 'phoned to say she wouldn't be able to come to see you today. Family crisis apparently."

Again.

"Another one, eh?" he said after a while.

"Yes," she said, looking embarrassed. "Another one."

"Ah well, at least I won't have to sit here listening to her lie about how well I'm looking and how much she's looking forward to me coming home."

The young woman squeezed his hand again.

"Yes," she said. "There is that I suppose. Never mind, small mercies and all that."

"Or silver linings."

"Better than dark clouds anyway," she said with a sad little smile.

She plumped the pillows and put the oxygen mask back over his mouth and nose. Then he watched her hip-sway and the movement of her legs under the tight blue uniform as she walked out of his room. Watched in the same way he would have done with the girls when he was fifteen. With exactly the same feelings of impossible longing and impotence.

Then he lay back, put his earphones in, replayed the song and thought about Geordie again. Not a bad way to go, he thought. Better that than being slowly monitored, drugged and doctored to death, anyway.

Happy birthday dad, he thought just before the monitor above his bed suddenly lost its waves and flatlined with a shrill, continuous beep. The nurses and doctors did their best but there was nothing they could do. The time of death was called and recorded.

His favourite nurse was inconsolable, and her boyfriend couldn't understand why. Even after she'd explained it. He didn't last long.

MOTHER'S RUIN

One

It was almost nine months before they found her body. Eight months, three weeks, four days and six hours since we'd reported her missing. A young Constable and an even younger WPC came to tell me. Male authority and the female touch. Too obvious.

Because I knew. Instantly. Before they said a word. The look on their faces sucked the breath from my body. Stopped my heart. Stopped time. I saw the uniforms and I just knew. Don't cry I told myself. Don't you dare. Not in front of these youngsters. Hand tight on the door to stay upright. No tears. Not now. The day finally arrives, and they send children to tell me?

Superintendents and Chief Inspectors they'd been back then. Back when she was the third child, girl, that is, to be taken by the 'Monday Maniac'. Because he took them on Mondays. That was the first label I saw. The red-tops never were original in their alliterative nonsense.

"Maniac". "Beast". "Animal". Terms all used by the media. Defining the supposed difference. Not like the rest of us, was what they meant. Because we can't accept that, can we? We'd have to look too closely into ourselves if we couldn't apply the labels and place them outside of us. Except, I knew he wasn't. He wasn't different. Wasn't an obvious animal. She wouldn't have gone with a maniac, a beast. She knew better than that. I'd taught her better than that.

He must be normal, I'd said. Look and sound normal. Otherwise, she wouldn't have gone with him. She was smart, aware. She wouldn't have let a maniac beast take her. Why couldn't they see that? No cloven hooves and brimstone breath on this one. It's Mr Average you should be looking for. She'd smile and talk to Mr Average. Well dressed and gentle. A dad man. A grandad man.

But they weren't interested. They didn't want to hear me unless I conformed to their victim line. Their female victim line. And on their cues as well. Which I did in the end when I lost the energy and will to oppose them. Way back then when the media were interested. Because she was the third. Famous by numbers, like fifteen minutes of fame. And because she was 'beautiful and talented'.

Thank God she wasn't fat, spotty with a hare lip then, I'd said to one of them, otherwise even the Daily bloody Star wouldn't have bothered turning up.

To shock them? Or shock myself out of the grey depths. Both, probably. But meaning it all the same. I shocked them even more when I refused their money. Big five figures to tell us your story, love. You won't have to write a word, we'll do all that, just tell us about your life. And Ellie. And your husband, of course.

'*Been called worse, love*' was all they said when I told them they were pond scum. Smiled and shook their heads in disbelief when they realised I was serious.

The young Constables looked at me oddly when I asked where I'd have to go, and when, to identify her. There's nothing to identify, really, the young woman said to me. They found her in a small grove of trees - in a shallow grave, you see, she said, looking at her colleague again. Found by somebody walking their dog. Bloody dog walkers, I thought. Why is it always them that discover the bodies? Couldn't we slash the murder rate if we just banned dog walking?

We did it from dentals, and DNA just to make sure, she said, bringing me back to everything I didn't want to face, to acknowledge. It's a skeleton, she said. Just bones. Animals and weather take everything except the skeleton. And the animals even take parts of that. So it's not a body to speak of. Not that you'd recognise.

It's not a "body", I said. A skeleton. It's Ellie. My daughter. What you've got now is nothing to do with physical form. It's my Ellie. Flesh of my flesh and blood of my blood. But they didn't understand. Left as soon as they could after telling me when I could arrange for an undertaker.

Two

I buried Ellie this afternoon. With nobody round the house afterwards. Church, grave, then fuck off. Left the 'fuck off' off the notices, of course, but I made sure the message was clear enough.

We reported her missing, I said. We. Because we had been 'we', then. Two of us. More numbers. Numbers that outline everything but ultimately mean nothing. Fifteen years knowing him. Twelve years married to him. Eleven years nurturing Ellie. Nine months without her. The beginning and the end.

Not 'we' now. Because he was gone within four months. Couldn't stand my silence he told me. My silence? You shit. Why can't you not stand the silence of Ellie not being here?

He looked at me as if I was mad when I finally said it. Talk to me, talk to me, he pleaded one night. In tears. But tears of his own futility, frustration and rage. Not tears for Ellie. Not tears of shared loss, shattered dreams and an empty future.

"How can I, when you've never let me talk to you in fifteen years?" I'd asked. "You've never wanted me to in fifteen years, never listened when I did talk, so why do you want me to start now? Because I don't know what you want me to say. All I know is you won't want to hear what I have to say, what I really want to say.

I can listen I'd told him. (Wondering if it's a woman thing, this ability to actually listen? To hear the chords as well as the melody?) I'm a very good listener now I'd said, because that's all I've ever done with you. It's always been all about you. You talked about work, your career, the house, mortgage, holidays, clothes, possessions and cars. Not about us. About our life together. Our shared dreams and hopes for Ellie. No, the truth is, you never experienced us at all. You experienced work, sleep, sex, football, cars, food and drinking with your mates. I just sat here all those years and listened. And talked to Ellie instead.

That was the hardest of all. The silence. More than talking to her. More than the missing touch, the missing kiss, it was the sounds I missed. The sounds before the touch and the kiss came. The silence was killing me. No more footsteps, no thundering on the stairs, no yelling from upstairs "Muuum! Where's me…" No music, no singing, no laughter, no tears. Nothing. A vacuum that can't ever be filled.

"You'll never get over it, but you'll get used to it eventually", the counsellor said.

But when does eventually come? And how can you get used to something that isn't? I asked him. You can get used to anything that is. If it's real, you know what you're dealing with, but how do you, with something that isn't?

He couldn't tell me. Just plastered me with platitudes. Another him. The 'Bereavement Counsellor' this time. Dealing in things he understood, not the things that I didn't. And he didn't seem to understand the difference. He was just another part of their standard procedures. Came in a thin plastic wallet like everything else the Police did.

"I'm not bereaved." I said. "Not yet. Maybe never. I don't know how to be bereaved when I haven't finally lost anybody. I looked it up in the dictionary. Ellie's. 'To widow, orphan, or deprive by death of some dear relative or friend'. That's what it says. But that doesn't apply to me. Yet. Because some fragment of my brain tells me she might not be dead. Other fragments tell me she is, but how can I know for certain? I can't. Not enough to be bereaved."

He said nothing. Just sat there in his carefully dishevelled clothes waiting for me to say something more. To 'talk about my feelings'.

'Earn your bloody money', I'd wanted to scream. Do what I need, not what you've been taught. Sod technique, I'm a person not a specimen. Not a reaction in a test tube. I don't know your words, your language. I've got an English Degree, but I don't begin to understand your language.

Feel? How do I feel? I can tell you in my words, but they've all been used and abused so much that they sound like clichés now. They are clichés. But they're all I know.

I don't know how to feel in your language. Distraught, angry, devastated and suicidal? All of those. So trite. So unclever. So talk with me. Don't ask questions and wait in silence for answers that connect to what you already know. Talk with me like my friends used to.

No need for counsellors then. Oh no. Not with my girlfriends around. Everything talked about and talked out. Nights of alcohol, chocolate and feelings laid bare. And taken care of. No girlfriends left now, though. Fifteen years of him put paid to them. All washed up on the dry beach of my husband's existence.

A husband who said I had to come to terms with it. 'You need to pull yourself together', he said.

"If I could find the edges, grab them and pull my arms around to do it don't you think I would!!"

I'd finally screamed.

Finally, because it was his last night in the house. Wanted me to talk to him, but he didn't know how to listen. Couldn't listen. Couldn't hear my words. Just frightened by the fact and sounds of them. Especially when the scream released something he'd never seen before, a part of me that terrified him.

He went then. The same day. I came home and he wasn't there.

Gone.

Without a word.

No letter.

No card.

No scribbled note.

No forwarding address.

Just an empty wardrobe and no CDs left.

And no contact since. Not even at the funeral despite me surprising myself by sending an invitation for his brother to pass on.

What happened to those fifteen years? When did fifteen add up to nothing? How is the sum of him, me, and Ellie, zero? What am I supposed to come to terms with there?

"Don't worry,' Kieran said. "It's gone, he's gone. His loss."

Kieran. The son of the Irish couple next door. Called to say he was sorry once the press had disappeared. Didn't want to say it before in case the bastards wanted a quote and he ended up punching one of the fuckers, he said.

I was shocked by someone speaking to me without filters. It shocked me awake.

"If that's his reaction, fuck him," Kieran said. You can cope better on your own 'cos you can take care of how you're feeling instead of having who you are now screwed over by him all the time."

How did he know? Eighteen years old and putting his hand right on it. Without wearing a glove, either.

Knocked on the door two weeks later and gave me a CD he'd done me, labelled "THE DARK."

What?

"Don't ask," he said, "just listen. Because it's funny, listening to desperate songs when I'm down always makes me feel better. Better than going to useless counsellors and support groups anyway."

Counsellors and support groups. He said it with total contempt.

All these singers and bands have been there, done that, got the t-shirts, he said. Helped him to feel he wasn't alone. That there were others in this world who had suffered just as much, and they were dealing with it. More than that, they'd turned their pain into something beautiful.

"I can't do that," he said. "Not clever enough. But I love the fact that it's possible."

And smiled. First person to smile in my presence in nearly five months. Played the first track. Something about feeling pain is better than no feelings at all. Exactly! First thing to make sense since we realised she was late.

"You need to deal with your guilt feelings," the Counsellor had said.

Guilt? What guilt? She was eleven. Bright. Aware. The shop was on the corner, forty yards away. Only forty yards but nine months travelling it. A single ticket to the grave. She went every night. Diet Coke or whatever drink was 'cool'. And sugar free gum. Little things, but every night. Like cleaning her teeth and brushing her hair. Familiar things. And you don't die from familiar things, do you? How can you die from forty yards? From habit? From familiarity?

Familiar acts are beautiful when done with love, I read somewhere once. Was his a familiar act to her? Did he take her through familiarity? Did she know him? Is that how he took her?

Not if I'd been there. No. But I wasn't, and all those things were thought. And said by others. To others. Never to my face.

"Where was she, then?"

"Imagine letting her out at that time of night."

"Only takes a second."

"Blink of an eye. In a flash."

"Think she'd know that, her being a teacher."

Never, "Where was he, the bloody husband?" Oh no, never that. We women, the nurturers, the carers and the cursed.

I'd feel much more guilty if I'd said no, and she died falling from her bedroom window trying to climb out and do it, I said to the counsellor.

"Why do you feel that?" he asked, peering at me over his counsellor's glasses. "It's a very interesting way to express it."

Interesting. God help me. The end of another 'meaningful exchange'.

Kieran didn't tell me he understood how I was feeling. Didn't pretend to. Just told me that if I felt like he did when his brother died of meningitis then I must feel worse than shite.

I almost laughed.

He comes every now and then. To listen to the desperadoes as he calls them. Played me one song about a woman who needed shooter, a killer. Oh yes. Shoot him down. Natural feeling, I was told. Really? Not for me. It takes some coming to terms with, me who's never been violent. Ever. Always opposed it. To know I could kill somebody without thinking about it. And now I know I could. Now that does need some coming to terms with. Not my bloody textbook guilt. Or lack of it. The textbook probably says that's psychopathic.

Hmmm. Even more interesting case, doctor.

That's not what I am. Like Edna, the inebriate, screaming at the court "I am not the vagrant", I am not a case!

Rage against the dying of the light. Or Rage Against the Machine, one of the bands Kieran played me. Gets me out of myself, he said.

Oh, yes. Yes, please. Take me. Far, far away from here.

And get me out of TV appeals. You never know, they said, it might just... experience has shown... these things often have a pattern.

Why can't they just admit they haven't got a clue. Just brought out their plastic wallets, opened the first one in the series and followed procedures.

Applied intelligence, they said. The collected knowledge of previous cases. And help from the public, the citizen, of course. That is crucial in cases like this.

But she's not previous, I'd said. Talking at them in a way that frightened me after years of not talking. This has never happened before. Ellie's never been taken before.

And where's the wisdom in all your procedures, your processes? How many cases have you solved by "following procedures?"

No answer.

And who are the guardians here? The solvers? The police or the citizen? Do you share your salary around the members of the public who help solve it for you? Your Superintendent's Super Salary? He just smiled at me. Patronisingly. Because collective plastic wallet knowledge told him that bereaved mothers, the women, often became irrational. Or hysterical. Or both. No, once they realised her father had nothing to do with it and there was no demonic stepfather on the scene (plastic wallet No. 2) they were clueless then.

They just opened up wallet No. 3 and followed all their pathetic, poly-procedures. Including the TV appeal. Satisfaction for all the masturbatory voyeurs.

Is he listening and watching? I asked.

Most probably, they said, experience has shown...

Then what exactly is the bloody point of asking for her safe return? I asked them. He didn't take her so he can hand her back. So why should he listen to me? As if he couldn't work out for himself what a Valium-dulled, grieving mother like me would say. And isn't it just possible that he *wants* a TV appeal? Wants to see me? So he can get some kick from that as well. Is that not more likely than him telling you where she is, I asked.

No answer. Just patronising smiles.

Why can't I say, "Just let me know where she is, you evil, murdering swine, so I can bury her? So I can do what I need to. You did what you needed to with her. Just let me do what I need to now. Or are you a selfish evil, murdering swine as well." Why would that not work just as well as appealing to him for her return, or at least her whereabouts? Why not?

Oh no. Unacceptable.

They just shook their heads and gave me the old, 'there, there' looks. Kept pressing me but I kept refusing. What's the point? Tell me that, explain it in a way I can understand, and I will. Otherwise, close your plastic wallets and leave me alone. They just shook their heads again and dismissed yet another irrational mother.

Closure. That's what you're seeking, what you need, they said. Kept on saying it even when I told them I didn't understand what they meant. Didn't think they really knew what they meant. Because there's no such thing, I said. It's not like closing a book for god's sake. She'll always be gone, that's a constant, not something you can close. Can't lock her memory away so it never intrudes. No closure. Just nothing. Numbness.

And remember it's not personal, she said. Not against you as a person. It's random. Neutral.

"Not personal? Takes my daughter, works out his particular form of sadism on her. Then most likely kills her? My Ellie? And it's not personal? Explain to me exactly what is personal, then you empty, patronising cow. I've an eighteen-year-old boy who's more use to me than you."

Spoken out loud for once. But with tears. Why do I cry when I finally have the courage to say what I think? Every time. Why?

End of second Counsellor 'relationship'. A woman this time. They said I'd relate better to another woman. That was when I finally understood they knew nothing. And worse, understood that I knew nothing either. Could do nothing. I struggled for it with Kieran. And we eventually found it.

Empty. That's the word. Sums it up. A huge piece of me gone. From my core. Void. It's real, but it's all cliché somehow. I miss her. There's an emptiness inside me. That's it and that's all of it. Everything. I... Miss... Her... The simplest thing we ever say about somebody. We miss them. And now the biggest ever. I miss her. It's huge. And I can't make it smaller. I can't not miss her.

Time will heal the priest had said.

How long? I asked.

That depends, he said, we're all different.

Then for God's sake, say something different to me!

Find your own words in that case, Kieran said. Say it yourself. So I tried.

And nearly made love to him last night. A boy. Almost had sex with him. Pure, raw and wild. As I once used to when I was a whole woman. Wanted to. So desperately. Right there on the front room sofa. Played it all in my mind. Imagined myself doing it. Felt myself doing it. Doing him. I even dared touch him. Just a little. Stroked his hair as I passed behind the chair. Then kissed the top of his head. He seemed to know. He Looked up at me.

"But would you still respect me in the morning?" he said with a smile. A nice smile. But he didn't touch me.

Oh, he knew.

He kissed me on the forehead when he left. Didn't say anything, just gave me a fleeting sweet kiss, smiled his quiet little smile, and left.

And I still would have then. I think. And he might have too. I think. If he'd touched me. But I needed him to take that step. Because I couldn't cross the line to make it so. Couldn't bring my mind to it. Too full of police, counsellors, priests and silence. And Ellie.

Three

Got to stop that. Got to concentrate. Stop my mind going everywhere. Just concentrate on the colour. Watch the colours.

I feel warm now. Funny, I thought I'd feel cold.

Surprisingly, it looks such a nice colour. Nicer even than the bubble bath Ellie bought me. Raspberry that was. My blood looks much darker than I thought, even when it's mixed with the bath water.

And I can hear better as well. I can even hear the central heating boiler rumbling away as, razor blade forgotten, I slide under the water.

STOP THE BUS

One

When the sun hit his face and woke him up he was lying under the front wheels of a number 11 bus. Knocked down? No, he thought, nobody's giving it the, "give him air, let him breath" stuff. And anyway, in a London Transport bus garage? Hardly. Couldn't begin to think how he came to be there at all. Apart from anything else, it hurt his head too much. Why under it? Why not inside the bloody thing? And why a number 11, anyway? The only bus he ever used was the 88, Clapham North to Trafalgar Square and back every day. Followed by a walk to the hell of the office on the one hand or the hell of home on the other.

Home! Oh Jesus. When was he last there? Found he had no idea. Couldn't remember the last time he saw his home and his wife. Sounds like a bad line from an even worse country and western song, he thought. No good, though. No good without a solid reference point. Find out what day it is first. That'd be a start.

He rolled carefully out from under the bus, checking his clothes and his body as he emerged and knelt on the concrete floor. Mid-grey, lightweight Burton's suit - well at least it's not Winter - cream button-down Ben Sherman and new red silk tie. And black shoes, the Ravels. Wednesday gear. So it must be Thursday, or later.

The oil patches matched the shoes but didn't exactly complement the suit. But at least there were no holes or tears in it. His watch was still in place - just seven o'clock according to that - but the glass seemed to him to be more scratched than usual. Or was that imagination? Nope. He noticed the knuckles of both hands were scraped and there was dried blood on his wrists, cuffs and shirt front. But whose? His own? How?

But later for all that. Later. There were much more important things right now. Such as, where exactly was he? What day of the week was it? And what was that bloody taste in his mouth. His mouth. Jesus. Tongue like a badger's arse. Got to stand up.

He put his hands on the front of the bus and gradually eased himself up. He rested his head against the radiator feeling the benefit of the cold chrome on his cheek. Christ! The pain running from his eyeballs to his neck and shoulders, blitzing his brain on the way, indicated a solid beer and spirit hangover. He stood still for a minute until the stars went and he could open his eyes again.

Searched his pockets for some clues. Keys. Okay, can at least get in when I get home... that's if she'll let me, of course. Penknife with can and bottle opener and thingummy for taking stones out of horses' hooves. Don't see many of those these days. Horses, that is. Pity, could've fancied doing an Androcles on Clapham High Street.

Telephone number scrawled on a page torn from a pocket diary. But was she tasty? Was it a she, even? And no paper money. Oh, great. He dug deeper. Less than a pound in coins and two Embassy in a crumpled packet. But no matches. Shit. A betting slip showing a yankee from Sandown and Catterick. Losers again, no doubt. A half-bottle in the inside jacket pocket.

Hundred and Twenty proof Jamaica Rum? Imported. Oh Christ, must have been drinking with the brothers again. Aye, fine. That narrows it down to half of South London, then. Bus pass safely in the top pocket. So, home or the office can be reached. Great. But which to head for? Weekday or weekend? Which? Easiest way's to find a paper shop. Oh ho! he thought, the old brain's beginning to function again. The Guardian and a bottle of Irn Bru would restore some much-needed balance. He turned towards the door.

"Oi! You!"

The unmistakable voice of petty authority. Coming from somewhere behind him.

"Oi!" Again. What is this now? Sounds like an English Sergeant Major in a Carry-On movie. He turned to see an Inspector at a side door.

"Yes. You there. You're not totally deaf then?"

Oh, a comedian as well.

"What the hell d'you think you're doing in here, eh? This is restricted, for staff."

And you're certainly restricted staff, pal. Five feet eight of nothing, uniform not so much worn as tattooed to his body. Cap attached by the bolts in his head, no doubt. He was coming closer now, getting brave because he'd noticed the suit, collar and tie.

Why do these people always assume if you're dressed like that it makes it safe? Don't they know that no self-respecting South London boy would ever go out of an evening in anything less than a £50 hand-stitched mohair? And hadn't he heard of the Krays? Best dressed bad bastards ever.

I really needed this, he thought as he shook his head. Don't you know I'm an absolute bear first thing in the morning?

"I said, what the hell d'you think you're doing in here?"

Milking cows, what does it look like, he thought, but couldn't get his mouth to say. Add Evo-Stick to the badger's arse.

"I'm talking to you. You dumb as well as deaf?"

Arsehole. Just Ignore him. He turned for the open doors and the sunshine beyond.

"I won't ask you again, sonny!"

No you fucking won't. But not for the reasons you think, pal. Sonny? You what? He turned around. The man was only three feet away. Oh, brave. Very brave. He took a deep breath and then poked the man's chest. Hard.

"Listen, pal, cos I'll only say this the once. If I knew for sure who I am, where I am, how I got here, what the fuck I'm doin' here, and what I was doin' last night and God knows how many nights before that, I'd tell myself first and then mebbe you, if only you'd asked me nicely. So I'm off now an' if I find out any of those answers I'll send you a fucking post card.

"A bloody Jock. I should have known. You're all the bloody... "

Ach, enough. The forehead on the nose cut the man short and sent the cap flying. The knee between the legs and the fist on the back of the neck put him down, moaning and retching into the concrete.

"And a single to Clapham North, please, conductor," as the unnecessary foot against the side of the head, twice, silenced the man completely. He rolled him over with his foot. Blood was running down his face and thicker, darker, blood oozed from his ears. He bent down and put his face close to the man's mouth. Hardly breathing, eh? If only I'd the balls to do that to the wife or my boss.

He felt for a pulse. Yep, there was, but very faint. Hope he doesn't have to rely on a bus coming along to save him. And then went through the man's pockets. A result. Came up with over seven pounds, sixteen Rothmans in a packet and a Ronson lighter. Which had no flint. Ach well, win some, lose some. Let's go find that paper shop.

Two

Two hours later, the Guardian had told him it was Saturday, the Irn Bru had restored his mouth and the packet of flints had delivered that first, sweet, nicotine hit of the day. Feeling somewhat refreshed, he walked down the steps to a basement flat in Clapham. His Jamaican neighbour, Charles, was just leaving next door. He didn't speak, just raised both eyebrows, smiled and walked off shaking his head. Christ, he thought, if it's reached Charles, it must be worse than bad.

"No, no, she doesn't not like you 'cos you're black" he'd said to Charles the first time they'd had a drink together. "It's not as simple as that".

He'd walked into this pub just past the railway bridge and found it full of West Indians. Even the barmen. Who looked at him like the bad guys looked at Randolph Scott when he walked into the saloon. But after the day he'd had, the sort of day only decent amounts of alcohol would even begin to cure, the familiar phrase, "a pint of Guinness an' a large Bells, sir," was spoken without a second thought. "Same again, please, bartender," just as the guy came back from the till with his change, brought a comment from his left.

"Man, you either had one bad day or you're well serious about this business."

"Both," he replied, with a laugh. "What you havin'?" and turned to see his neighbour from next door's basement flat. A guy he'd seen a few times during the six months he'd lived there, but never spoken to. Worked shifts. Never been sober when he'd seen the guy so never sure it was the same one next time. But it was him this time, raising a near empty pint of Guinness.

The question and the fresh pint that followed got him a seat at a table and an introduction to three of his neighbour's friends. Laid back guys, all Zoot suits and pork-pie hats. Out of date, sure, but still looking cool on them. They were all late thirties, early forties, like Charles, but more wary, trying to work him out.

Check it out. White, sure, we know white! English? No. English polite says, "would you care for a drink?" not, "what you havin'?"

Scottish?

"No. Glasgow, man, there's a big difference."

Hmmm. File that one away for future reference. Him 'ave no problem drinkin' in this pub. Well relaxed. Work? Suit and tie say office, eyes say different. Married? Ring say yes, behaviour say different. Check it out, man. Offered him a leather jacket. Worth Fifty quid. To him, a spar of Charles, only ten.

Be subtle guys, eh?

"No thanks guys. I'm allergic to leather." "Yeah," he says, "I've noticed, every time I wake up an' I've still got my shoes on, I've always got a blindin' headache."

And they liked it. Old ones are always the best. Worked a treat and they all relaxed. Till one of them mimicked his accent.

"Hey! What's yer name again? Clive, is it? Don't do that, okay, Clive? I don't try'n talk like you, don't go "ras clartin" all over the place like some racist comedian, do I? So don't you with mine. Okay?"

In a quiet, but serious voice. Which got them looking at each other and nodding. Then at him. With what? Respect? If not, then a different view, certainly. But no resentment because the conversation picked up again right where they'd left off. At least he assumed it did. Because the more they drank, the more they slid into Jamaican patois. Sober he might have had some chance staying with it. Drunk, he'd none. Just listening to the sounds was nice though. Voice music.

And then they were alone, just the two of them, Charles asking him why he was drinking with a Black man his wife looked right through every time she saw him.

"No, no, that's not the reason at all." Desperate to reassure a new-found drinking partner. "No. See, if you were a consultant at Guy's... a partner in a firm of solicitors... and Black, she'd have your babies. She's colour blind. Really. You're undesirable 'cos you're working class, that's all. And Blue-Collar workin' class as well. You work on the Underground, man. As a guard. A driver might get you the occasional "good morning" if she was in the right mood. But a guard? And your wife's a school dinner lady? Christ, she didn't even speak to them when she was five years old! That's why. Nothin' to do with the colour of your skin. She'd be exactly the same if your skin was white. Seriously."

Trying to explain petit bourgeois Scottish snobbery to a forty-year-old Jamaican who was still trying to work out the nuances of the English class system after twenty years living in London.

"See, she's worse than that, 'cos she doesn't even not like you. Sayin' she didn't like you'd be admittin' to some kind of human recognition, emotion even. No, far as she's concerned, you just don't exist man." Trying to get the message right through the haze of six Jamaica Rum that had followed Guinness and whisky in a steady flow.

Rum? Hundred proof? No problem. My mother used to feed me whisky in my bottle as a baby. "Same again bartender."

Problem was it made him drunk, but not Charles. He seemed to have some sort of immunity. He ends up talking shite and Charles just sits there smiling.

"What you need to understand, Charles, nobody's a person to her like they are to you an' me, like most of the rest of humanity. They're only what they do, what they are. An' if that doesn't fit what she unnerstands, what she likes an' approves of, she goes blind. Doesn't see you. And doesn't need to. She can smell an undesirable six carriages away in the rush hour Tube. And think's it's disgraceful the Tube hasn't got first class carriages. She went to Uni' as well. Degree in Sociology. PhD in how to identify and avoid contact with lower social orders. Can always tell I've been drinkin'. How? By the smell, same as your wife does with you? Nope. She says it's because my accent always *descends*. But it's not really her fault. See this is a woman who was raised by a mother who judges people's parentage, upbringing, education, character, values and social standing by the sort of wallpaper they've got on their dining-room walls. Whose greatest regret in life's she wasn't born an Edinburgh protestant."

Charles laughed and shook his head.

"A mother who thought I was good enough for her daughter 'cos I wiped my feet when I went in her house first time, said please and thank you and called a sandwich, a sandwich, not a "piece". And a father who is the third deputy temporary assistant manager of a two-window branch of the Royal Bank of Scotland. With a house you can see Bearsden from."

Charles really looked puzzled now.

"Unnerstan' what I'm sayin' here? She's a woman who can spot a moved ornament quicker than she can spot a dropped aitch. Won't allow you to drink out of a can watchin' the telly. A woman who won't hang her underwear out in public. Who can have a three day moody 'cos you left the toilet seat up again. If useless fuckin" knowledge about how people are supposed to behave was gold, I'd be able to buy Jamaica."

"She fucks good, though."

"What?" A third of his pint was coughed across the table. Startin to seriously like this man. "Charles. I was expectin' some reaction to that little speech. But 'Scuse me?"

"Man, you want screw your woman summer nights, close the window. She commentates better than Peter O'Sullevan. Stopped the party in the garden last week quicker than a visit from the police."

"Oh! Oh aye. Weird but, innit? Can't work it out meself. Doesn't admit to havin' periods, won't even say the words penis or vagina, won't allow swearin' in the house, but her language in bed's amazin'. Well, you know. You've heard her."

"So, you don' like her much but you like to fuck her?"

"Yep. Spot on that is, Charles. Succinctly put my man."

"So why marry a woman you don' like? Y'ave no chil'ren, can't 'ave bin pregnant."

Aaaah, slipping in the easy ones after six pints, eh? "I don't know, Charles. Except she asked me and I couldn't think of a good reason not to. Pissed at the time of course. Me that is, not her."

Which brought laughter, two more pints and rums, and a nightmare stagger back to the flat with Charles as his only solid reference point. And a week in Siberia after the Guinness and rum was deposited all over the bathroom. How was he supposed to know she'd cleaned it while she waited for him to come home?

Three

He smiled at the memory. Still, he thought, if it means she's finally spoken to Charles it can't be all bad, as he took a bunch of keys from his pocket and managed to find one that fit the lock. He paused, closed his eyes and took a deep breath before turning the key.

There were no lights on and the flat was warm and silent when he walked into the hall. He got no answer when he called his wife's name, so he checked each room in turn. The place was immaculate, as ever, but there was no sign of her in the lounge or the bathroom. Where he washed his hands to get rid of the blood. No sense giving her a ten-point start. By the time he reached the kitchen, his heart was pounding, and he half expected to find a note from her saying she'd finally left. But there was nothing on the table apart from a blue and white checked tablecloth. And last night's meal.

His meal. Spaghetti bolognese, congealed in a bowl set in his place at the table. With a clean wine glass, fork, spoon and serviette arranged perfectly around it. And a bread roll, two knobs of butter and a knife on a side plate. The bowl of grated Parmesan, with its proper wee silver spoon, sat alone in the centre of the table. Her stuff all washed up and put away. Naturally. The empty wine bottle in the bin. He left it all where it was, turned and put the Irn Bru in the fridge. And smiled. Be fun when she finds that in there. R Whites Lemonade? Cans of Coke or 7 Up? Fine. But a screw-top bottle of Irn Bru?

"Not in here. In my house. Only common people drink that. It used to have a lot of iron in it years ago so that the children of poor people didn't get Ricketts. I think we've progressed beyond that, John, don't you?" As she turned a harmless bottle of pop into an unexploded bomb.

He went to the bedroom and there she was, propped up on the pillows with a cup of coffee, reading a paperback. She didn't look up as he leaned against the doorpost. He stood quietly, looking at her, realising he'd have to break the silence.

"Hi darlin', he said. "Want a fresh coffee?" She didn't reply or even look up. Just turned a page. Fuck.

"You alright?" he asked, not daring to enter the room. She just carried on reading.

"Lisa? You okay?" But she still didn't look up from her book when she spoke. "I don't know who you are, how you know my name or what you think you're doing in my flat," she said. "But if you don't leave right now, I'm calling the police."

"Aw c'mon Lisa, don't be like..."

"Don't be like what? I'll be exactly how I like, thank you very much. And I'll tell you exactly why. See, I used to live here with my husband, but he disappeared over two days ago. Never knew when he was coming home most times, mind, never the most reliable man I've ever met, but he was never gone for over two days before. And I don't know why I should, since he obviously doesn't give a damn about me, but I've been going out of my mind with worry. More fool me, I suppose."

At least she's talking, he thought. Even if it is right through me. Chances, chances. But he still didn't dare enter the room.

"I 'phoned his office but he hasn't been there for two days and he hasn't called them either. They were not happy. Will called round last night because he hadn't seen or heard from him either. So I 'phoned the Police but he's not been arrested, not under his own name anyway. I even checked the hospitals but he's not there. So, he's either lying dead somewhere or he's gone and left me. I wouldn't wish him dead, of course, but I really do wish he'd just bugger off out of it."

"Sorry. I really..."

"Funny. You know you sounded just like him then. He was always saying things he didn't mean as well. Thought saying them was enough. But it's not. Not then, not now. I keep thinking, if he'd really been sorry, if he cared at all, he would've rung me. Not too much to ask, after all. A few coppers in one of those red boxes they provide."

There was a long silence which he decided he'd better not break.

"So don't give me your usual chat, John. Not again. Not ever. I don't want to hear it. So just bugger off and leave me alone."

She finally looked up at him and the expression on her face said more than the words.

"Okay, okay. I know you're upset an' I don't blame you. I've been an arse."

"I've already got one of those, thank you, don't need another. So again, why don't you just bugger off."

"Yeah. Okay. I know there's not much I can really say..."

"Again."

"Okay! Again. But it wasn't what you think, it wasn't another woman..."

"Oh really? Well, that's a shame. I'd hate to think I'm the only member of my sex has to take shit from you. You could share it out a bit more, you know. You, the great bloody socialist, you could try practising what you preach."

"Okay, okay. It's just... it might be more serious this time, I don't know."

"As the old saying goes, you seem to have mistaken me for someone who gives a shit," she said. Said slowly, with heavy emphasis on every word.

Fuck, fuck.

"Okay Lisa. Have it your way. But there's a slim chance it might be serious. And a slimmer one they might want to talk to me. So, if the Police do call, just tell them you haven't seen me."

"Well, that won't be a lie, will it?" she said, not reacting to the suggestion of an official visit. "Wouldn't be able to get me for perjury on that one now, would they?"

"Aw, look. Lisa? Okay, tell you what, I'm goin' out for a bit..."

"Well that'll make a bloody change."

"... and we'll talk about it later."

"No we won't."

"But I wanted to..."

"You want to talk? Really? Because that's one thing you're good at, talking. Makes you feel better, is that it? Well talk to your bloody self, for a change. See if that eases your conscience... always supposing you can recognise that when you find it, that is."

"Okay, I get the message. Tell you what, I'll 'phone Will up, let him know you're in need of another counsellin' session... "

"You bastard!"

He turned and ducked as the book bounced off his shoulder and the coffee cup shattered against the door. Hope it was empty. Stains on the carpet are a bigger sin than adultery round here. No absolution for that one. He heard her shouting something about a guy coming round to change the locks, so he needn't think he'd get back in, but he was halfway out the front door by then. Ah well, he thought, as walked up onto the street, plenty money, anyway. And fags. Might as well go find the boys. Chelsea at home to Everton this afternoon. Should be a bit of a game. And the result should be a bit closer than the one that's just finished as well.

Four

It was half past twelve when he walked into the pub and spotted Will at a corner table reading the Sporting Life, his first pint almost dead. And dressed for the game. Nice clean, pressed, checked shirt, and beautifully ironed Levis. Spends more time with an iron in his hand than my mother ever did, he thought. And she had four of us. Plus my old man. Wearing trainers that looked like they'd just come out of the box. And a padded jacket neatly folded on the seat next to him.

He bought two pints of Guinness and took them across to the table. He smacked the paper with the back of his hand and sat down.

"What the...!! Christ, John, where the hell have you been? I've been trying to get you. Lisa had no idea where you were when I spoke to her yesterday. Tried your office as well. Where have you been the last two days? Where were you last night?"

"No idea. Both times."

"What? No idea?"

"Nope. None at all."

He lit a cigarette and took a first, long, drink. Will studied him.

"Jesus, you look like shit, John. You sleep on a park bench or what?"

"Come on, outdoors dressed like this? No, I woke up in a bus garage."

"A bus garage? Yeah, that'll be right. You don't want to tell me her name, okay, but don't sit there and take me for an idiot."

"No. Straight up. It wasn't a girl... at least I'm pretty sure it wasn't. Must've kicked me out very early if it was. But, like I told you, I woke up this morning in a bus garage. Got thrown out by an Inspector - well he tried to anyway."

"Tried to?"

"Yes. Well... actually we did discuss the situation but there was no meeting of minds, so I left of my own accord, as they say."

"So you hit him." Not a question.

"What makes you say that?"

"Because it's your default response to most things cause you a problem. Somebody tries to stop you doing what you want? You hit them. It's just you. Has been as long as I've known you. Even I do a runner when I see the red mist rising."

"Okay, yeah. Well, maybe I did give him a smack."

"I know your smacks. Is he okay?"

"How would I know, Will? I didn't exactly hang around for an ambulance or the police, now did I?"

"So it could be bad?"

"Not half as bad as having to sit here listening to all your preaching, Will."

"Somebody has to tell you..."

"Somebody has been telling me, though. Everybody's been telling me. All my bloody life. My mother, my older sisters, the nuns, priests, teachers, policemen. And now my wife. And you. You've never stopped telling me. The only one who ever made sense was my grandfather.

"You'll grow out of it John, son. Most boys do. And if you don't, well, you're the one that has to live with the worst consequences. Just learn to pick the right battles, that's all." And he was a better man than you and me will ever be, Will, so give me a break and just shut up about it. Okay?"

He took a long pull on his pint, lit a cigarette and stared over at the bar. Waiting for Will to break the silence. Which he knew he would. Wouldn't dare leave it too long. Be too worried I might not love him anymore.

"So. You were in a bus, then?"

He almost burst out laughing. "No, no Will. Not in a bus. On the garage floor, in front of a number 11."

Right from the top, he thought. Will's nothing if not a man for the detail. Got to have the far end of every bloody thing. Tell it once, tell it all and get it over with.

"Why not in a bus, though. It's nicer inside. Warmer. And the seats aren't too bad. 'Specially the long back ones downstairs you can lie on."

"What are you, an Estate Agent for London Transport? I'm not looking to buy a bloody double-decker, Will. Like I told you, I haven't a clue why."

"But how the hell did you come to be there in the first place?"

"Jesus Will. Ask me the easy ones, eh? If I don't know where the hell I've been for two days, how am I supposed to know why I ended up in a bus garage?"

Will just shook his head and took a mouthful of Guinness. "Shame of it is, you missed a good night. Well, eventually it was. I called round to see Lisa first, early on, see if she'd heard from you, but of course she hadn't. Then we all waited for you in the Spread Eagle. Till closing. Remember you were supposed to meet us in there to go on to that party in Battersea?"

Okay, just ignore the direct mention of the better half.

"Party? Battersea? Nope. Not even now you mention it, Will. And I certainly didn't last night. Obviously."

"Obviously. We waited 'til half-ten, but Macey said you wouldn't turn up."

"Yeah, he would. No, don't remember the pub, or the party. Don't even remember drinking this," he said, reaching into his jacket pocket and placed the empty half bottle of Rum on the table. Will picked up the bottle and studied the label.

"Rum? Since when did you drink Rum?"

He shrugged. "Since last night?"

"And a hundred and twenty proof? You might as well drink meths. Christ John, you've got to stop drinking."

"What for?"

"Because you've got a problem, that's why."

"A problem? Me? Not at all."

"Yes you bloody have. Be sensible. When you can't remember what you've done the night before, or where you've been for two days, that is a problem."

"Not necessarily, Will. It might be more of a problem if I could remember. Maybe it's so bad the old unconscious is doing me a favour by blocking it out."

Will shook his head and took another pull on his pint.

"Been to the flat yet?"

"Of course, soon as I was up. Went home to get some breakfast and a change of clothes."

"Lisa there?"

He laughed. "Talk silly. Of course she was. Why'd you think I'm starving and still look like shit."

Will shook his head yet again and stubbed out his cigarette.

"She still upset? She was last night."

"Wouldn't you be?"

"You know I would. But doesn't it bother you at all?"

"Of course it does, Will. Jesus!"

"Why d'you do it, then?"

John sighed. "Look, I don't *do* it, Will. Not deliberately, I mean. It just seems to happen. Don't mean to, don't plan it, sit there all day at work thinking up ways to upset Lisa. It's not to have a go or anything. It just happens. Then I realise afterwards it wasn't the right thing to have done, you know? Not exactly the brightest way to behave. I just know I got it wrong again."

"I don't know how she puts up with you sometimes. She complains to me every time..."

"Yeah, I know."

"You know? How?"

"How? What d'you mean how? She bloody tells me, you arse. That's how."

"Oh! I didn't know that."

John shook his head and made a growling sound. "For a bright guy, you're awfully dumb sometimes Will. Of course she tells me. That's the whole point of it. Telling me every time what a nice guy you are, what a bastard I am in comparison. How she's complained to you, how you're such a good listener, such a good man. I tell her you only listen so well because you haven't a clue what to say, your vocabulary's so limited."

"You don't mind?" Will asked.

"What, your limited vocabulary?"

"Fuck off you. You don't mind she talks to me and complains about you?"

"Listen Will, tell me, why d'you think a woman tells all her troubles to a nice guy like you instead of one of her mates, another woman?

"I dunno, sympathy, I suppose."

"Sympathy? Not a chance. No, she'd be too worried she'd lay it on too thick, they'd think she was really pissed off with me and try to get me into bed."

Will snorted. "You arrogant bastard. It's not as if you're Robert Redford."

John laughed. "No I'm not. Never thought I was. But not ugly, Will. Not ugly. Looks don't seem to matter that much anyway. Some women always think they can reform a bastard, see it as a challenge. First step's always listen to his problems. As long as it takes for him to pour it all out. Next step's bed. Give him great sex and somehow they'll think he'll change. Never fails to get them underneath you, Will. You should try it sometime."

"So bloody sure of yourself, aren't you?"

"Only because I'm talking from personal experience, Will. I've screwed one already."

"What? You never told me. Who?"

"Jen."

"Jen?" Will said. Outraged. "But she's her best friend for God's sake."

"And your point is?" John said, smiling inwardly at his friend's naivety. Wondering how he'd got so far knowing so little. Must have studies all the time at Uni and missed out on all the students' shenanigans.

"You know exactly what I mean," Will said. "Screwing your wife's best friend? You really are a bastard, you know that, John?"

"So? Been told that before, by women as well." He shrugged and lit another cigarette. "It takes two, as they say, and I'm not into rape, never have been. And I don't remember having to threaten Jen or anything. Anyway, women are no different to us blokes, really. We just think they should be, for some reason. Or guys like you do. With the double standards you operate.

You know the old expression, "a stiff cock has no conscience"? Well, there's a female equivalent. Don't know what it is, but there has to be. Because a lot of women are just the same as us guys. They'll get up to all sorts of naughties if they think there's a good chance of not getting caught."

He smiled to himself as he saw Will shaking his head in disgust. Mothers, sisters, wives. *nice* girls and tarts. That's how Will classified women. With Aunties and Grans somewhere in mix. There were certain things that nice girls just didn't do.

"The other thing is, Will, she has to be able to use it against me. No point in her telling me she's been moaning to her friends, or her sister, is there? What do I care? But another man? My best mate? No, that's different."

He took a drink and lit another cigarette as Will stared at the far wall.

"Or she thinks it is. No. There's no point unless a woman can use it as a weapon against the bastard. And in this case, she happens to be the woman and the bastard happens to be me. And I accept that's what I am."

"And you really don't mind?"

"Mind? Not at all. Why should I?"

"You're worse than a bastard. She deserves better than you."

John laughed and pointed at his friend. "Deserves you, you mean? Forget it, Will, you've no chance."

Christ, he's blushing. John almost burst out laughing. Touched a little nerve, have we? Well let's just see where this goes.

"I didn't mean that," Will said. "I just meant... you treat her like some kind of unpaid servant, treat the flat like a hotel with room service. You just do what you want, and she tags along. Except you do most of it without her. I would never treat her like that."

"That's exactly my point, Will. You wouldn't treat her like I do, you'd bore her to bloody death. Look. We've been married three years. She's never left me, not for a night, never come near it, never screwed anybody else - and plenty've tried, so what does that tell you?"

There was a lengthy pause while Will thought about the question. What's so difficult about that, John wondered. Thought I'd fed him an easy one.

"I don't know. What?" Will eventually said.

"She must like it. She must like a bastard. I have absolutely no idea why. Most women don't. I've learned that some do though, and she's one of them. And she loves complaining. It's part of the attraction, being able to witter on to my mate about what a complete bastard I am, how I don't treat her with respect and what a hard life she has with me. She's like hypochondriacs, always the centre of attention when there's something wrong with them. She gets sympathy and attention when she's telling everybody what a bad life she's got with me. If it's so bad, why doesn't she leave?"

"She wouldn't, she's too loyal."

John laughed. "Loyal! You make her sound like a bloody dog. Faithful to its master. But it's not very loyal pouring her heart out to you, is it?"

He looked hard at his friend, but Will just took another drink and said nothing. Oh let's twist again, he thought. Just in the mood for it today. Have a go at me about my marriage? I'll bury you deep, you silly bastard. All aboard for fun time.

"Still, if it makes you feel good, Will, that's okay."

Will stared at him. "What d'you mean makes me feel good?"

"Oh come on, Will. You fancied her yourself, but you couldn't pull her, hard as you tried. But I did. Easily. And then suddenly, there she is, crying on your shoulder, your arm round her, making her feel better. Making you feel better, hoping it'll eventually lead you into her knickers. But it won't, Will. She won't ever let you. And not because you're my best mate, it's because you'd bore her to death, like I said. See, you're just too bloody nice. Too comfortable. No excitement at all."

"What are you on about, too nice? She likes that. Nice guys. She told me."

John burst out laughing. "Oh what! I can't believe you, sometimes, you're unreal. Into mutual fantasising the pair of you?"

"*If only I'd got together with a nice guy like you, Will, when I'd the chance, somebody who treats me decent, instead of a bastard like him. I wonder where we'd be now?*"

"Is that how it goes, eh? The pair of you mentally strolling into wonderland. How's Alice, by the way?"

Will stared down at the table, not daring to look at him and too embarrassed to say anything.

"You might well look embarrassed you silly sod. She's just winding you up. Don't you get it? She likes you, really, she just can't resist it. You just can't see her properly. This is one scheming woman, Will. She only likes "nice" when she wants to like it. I told you, what she really likes is bastards. Like me. I treat her like shit and she complains but she's still there, isn't she? Christ, I couldn't blame her if she did bugger off and leave me. Nobody could."

"You're right there."

"Yes, but she doesn't, does she? She always gives me a hard time and then cries on your shoulder, sure, but she never leaves, does she? Because she's just one of these people always needs something to complain about. And if there isn't anything, which is not often, grant you that, the way I carry on, she has to invent it. Like her total obsession with cleanliness and tidiness. When she needs one, and there's nothing else I've done, that one's always good for a row."

"But you are an untidy bastard. I remember when you and me shared the flat," Will said as he started shredding a beer mat in frustration.

"Will, Will. I know I am. Okay? I know it and she knows it as well. I walk in the bedroom, trip over my trousers, shirt... or shoes or something and I think "fuck me, you're an untidy bastard." But do I turn round and pick anything up and put it away? No."

"So no wonder she has a go, then."

"For God's sake, that's not why she does it. How many times do I have to explain it? Look, I'm twenty-six. Of course I know I'm an untidy bastard. But telling me all the time doesn't make me a tidy one, does it? And she knows that. She's not stupid. She'd absolutely hate it if I was tidy. So it's got sod all to do with me, with tidiness, it's all to do with her needing something to complain about. And somebody to complain to. So she complains about me. To you. My best mate. Nice. Safe."

"You bastard, John. I'm not a bloody eunuch, I'm not that safe." The beer mat was in pieces by now.

"Of course you are Will. No offence, but you're as safe as houses. That's the reason she talks to you. But she doesn't want safe and reliable. That's why you'll never get inside her knickers. Because if she does leave, it'll be for a bigger bastard, a worse one. Not a nice guy like you. So don't worry about it making you feel good. It's okay, you're my mate. If she's going to, and Christ knows I've given her enough reason, I'd rather she was there with you, moaning on, than out screwing some other guy."

"Honestly, the way you talk," Will said. "And she's a great girl as well."

"Yeah, I know that... well, most of the time she is."

"If you know how good she is, how much she loves you, and you love her, how can you treat her like this? It doesn't make any sense."

"It's easy. I'm an existentialist."

"Aaah, talk sense, will you."

"Okay then. Forget Marcel…"

Will frowned. "Marcel? What are you on about?"

"Gabriel Marcel. The guy who coined the phrase 'existentialism'. No?"

Will shook his head. Just looked puzzled.

"I forget," John said. "You did English. What would you know about French Catholic philosophers? But forget all that," he said draining his pint. It's your shout so go get them in. Does that make more sense to you?"

Will shook his head again as he stood up and took the empty glasses to the bar. Witless bastard, John thought as he picked up the Sporting Life and checked out the betting slip he'd found. He's a good guy and an even better mate, but Jesus Christ! He'd been hung up on Lisa since that first night in the pub when they'd moved in on two women. When he'd taken Lisa home, leaving Will with her sister. He refused to see how manipulative she could be. The poor bastard didn't realise Lisa just laughed at him every time. And wouldn't believe it if he told him. She came back one time and said Will was the only guy she'd ever seen get an erection just from listening to her talk. And not dirty talk, either. He'd noticed she was always wild in bed after those little chats though. Maybe Will should become a sex therapist. Now there's a thought. He looked up and saw him coming back with two fresh pints and a hot steak pie.

"What's this?" he asked, pointing at the plate.

"What's it look like? You said you were starving, hadn't had any breakfast."

"See you," he laughed as he picked up the knife and fork. "Brown sauce as well. You'll make somebody a wonderful wife, one day. But would only be her you'd have to be nice to though, Will, not me."

"You sarcastic bastard."

"That's me alright," John said, tucking in. "But you know what I wish, Will? Just for a change, I wish people would tell me things about myself I didn't already know. That way I might start to learn something."

"So, you tell me something instead," Will said. Intense now. Leaning right forward over the table.

"Oh, here we bloody go. You want to let me finish this pie first?"

"Why did you marry her?"

"No, thought not," John said. "What was that again?"

"I said, why did you marry her in the first place if you don't give a toss?"

"Because she told me we were."

"Told you you were, what?"

"That we were getting married. She told me."

"But you must have asked her. How else could she have agreed?"

"That's what I thought. One night we were both very drunk and next morning, all of a sudden she's telling me about the kind of ring she wanted, the sort of wedding she'd have, inviting her parents and all the rest of the family, who did I want to invite and how thrilled she was I'd asked her to marry me. So I thought, well, Jesus, I must've asked her. What would you have thought, eh?"

Will shook his head. "But you can't remember? Seriously?"

John finished his pie and took a long drink of Guinness. He laughed. "I can't even remember ever discussing the subject in the abstract, never mind coming right out and asking her the direct question. At first I kept trying to remember, re-running whole weeks, but then I thought what's the point? Really. What is the bloody point? You know her, Will, say what you like about her but she's honest, so I guessed she was telling me the truth. I must've been drunk or stoned or something."

He paused because a man at the next table asked if he could have a quick look at the Sporting Life. John handed it to him, and the man quickly checked the tip of the day and gave it back.

"Where was I now?" John said.

"The phantom wedding," Will said.

"Ah yeah, the wedding. All I could think was, she's telling me, so I must've asked, she's dead keen, got a good job earning decent money, my family all like her, she's a great cook, she's tasty, goes at it like a rabbit on speed, stag night's an excuse to get totally rat-arsed without her giving me a hard time about it, I don't have to get involved making any of the arrangements just turn up on the day. So why the hell not?"

Will shook his head. "Tell me John, do you enjoy any of it?"

He looked at his friend and grinned. Oh well, let's take him all the way.

"Is the sex okay, that what you're asking?"

"No! I didn't," Will said, blushing again. "I didn't mean that at all."

"Yes you bloody did. You should see your face! Wouldn't talk to any of your friends about this if you were the one married to her, would you Will? But it's okay, you can ask, I don't mind. Put it this way, the way she goes at it, takes control, it's even easier than using your right hand."

"Easier?"

"What?"

"Easier, you said. Than having to use your right hand. You mean better?"

"No. Easier's what I said. Easier's what I meant."

"Fuck off."

"Fuck off? You're one for intellectual debate eh, Will? You and your English degree, I can hardly keep up with you. But tell me this, honestly, does having it away with a woman, any woman, give you cramp in your right arm?"

"That's not the point, though."

"Yes, it is. That's exactly the point. And it's a hell of a lot easier when someone else's doing it for you. With her hand or her mouth. But 'specially when she's on top. Our Lisa loves that. Then it's brilliant. And she's not at all obsessed with cleanliness and tidiness where oral sex is concerned, I'll tell you that for nothing. I'm not allowed to eat biscuits in bed because of the mess and crumbs, but she'll go down on me without a second thought? Is that weird or what? So I just lie there with my fantasies while she does all the work. Absolutely brilliant."

"You're sick, John, you know that?"

"No," he laughed. "Not yet. But I'm working on it, Will. I'm working on it. And talking of working on it," he said picking up the Sporting Life, "anything you fancy at Haydock, today?"

Five

They all went for more drinks after the game - naturally - and then on for a curry. All of which meant that it was half past one in the morning when he got back to the flat. And he was very, very drunk. At first he thought the drink was the reason he was finding it so difficult to make the key work until it dawned on him that it wasn't his lack of co-ordination, it simply didn't fit any more.

Fuck! he thought. She really has changed the locks.

Which indeed she had. And he never got back in again. Ever. He dossed with Will until the divorce came through and the settlement meant he could afford a place of his own.

Lisa never sees John anymore. She heard he got fat and drinks a lot. Guinness, probably.

THE QUIET MAN

One

I was seven years old before I realised that the world wouldn't always stay the same. The day it changed forever came when the quiet man disappeared.

Until then, the people and places all seemed fixed in time. My parents – especially my mother – my older brother, my grandparents, my aunts and uncles, the group of children from the street that I walked to school with, the teachers at the school itself and the parish priest at the church we attended. Even the shopkeepers in the village, they all remained the same.

The street I lived in, the house I woke up in every morning, the shops in the village, the school buildings and the church never changed. It was an ever-constant, reassuring, comforting and safe environment, where everybody knew everybody else, and they all looked out for one another. A great time and place to grow up in but I'm not sure it was the best preparation for life in a world that once it began to change, never seemed to stop.

The other constants were the social events and rituals. My parents were ballroom dancers and once a month they went to a formal dance in a ballroom in town. My mother would wear one of her three ball gowns. All were strapless, nipped at the waist and slightly flared to mid-calf. A black one for the formal dances and two others, one in emerald green, the other in dark red, for the more 'frivolous' occasions. I never did work out what made one dance 'formal' and another 'frivolous', but the difference was quite clear to my parents and their friends. Yet another part of the impenetrable mystique of adulthood when you are a small child.

My father would wear his black suit with the satin stripes down the legs, white shirt, black bow tie and patent leather dancing shoes. And always a flower in his buttonhole on special occasions. With fresh Brylcreem on his hair, cigarettes in one side pocket, lighter in the other, he was ready to go. They looked immaculate and I only realised in later years that my mum was actually quite beautiful.

They were invariably accompanied by another couple, Reginald and Irene, who always collected my parents in their car. Apart from the occasional brandy at Christmas, Reginald didn't drink, so my parents never had to suffer the expense of taxis to and fro. Reginald and Irene lived up the street from us but in the different world that existed above the dividing line between our council estate and the larger, more secluded private houses. Theirs was a four-bedroom house, with a garage, and it was quite different from any other house I had ever been in. Ours was clean but untidy. As were those of my friends. There were family photographs on the walls. Books, newspapers and magazines were in every room. Clothes and shoes were in evidence, along with piles of clothes awaiting ironing.

My brother and I kept our bikes in the space underneath the stairs from which would spill our football and cricket gear. There were little chips and scrapes in the paint in every downstairs room, so our houses looked a bit worn and lived in. Comfortable. But not theirs.

Even at seven years of age, I was always surprised when I went into their house because it was all quite alien to me. To begin with, everyone had to take their shoes off by the front door, something I had never experienced anywhere else. Every room was unbelievably tidy with absolutely nothing out of place and there were no pictures on the walls. In fact there was no evidence that anyone actually lived there. It all just felt very cold and empty.

The kitchen work surfaces were clear; even the kettle and teapot were kept in a cupboard until needed. All the rooms had fitted carpets where ours, and those of all our friends, had large, cheap rugs over the floorboards. And you only had to look around the place to know they didn't have any children.

My aunt once said she was convinced that Irene spent her days cleaning windows, polishing everything in sight and hoovering every single carpet. As well as writing lists for herself of the chores that needed doing on a daily basis. And never, ever hanging her underwear out on the washing line for the neighbours to see.

The garden was the same. There was no vegetable plot and all the flowers seemed to know their place. The lawn looked exactly like their carpets with the edges perfectly trimmed and not a daisy or dandelion in sight.

As well as the dances, Regionald and Irene were also regulars at the card games at our house. Along with an aunt and uncle, they would play cards on a Friday night, twice a month. Which is how I first came to meet them. The two couples would arrive at seven o'clock for hands of Rummy, Whist, Solo and then Bridge, and I was always there to say a dutiful goodnight before I was sent off to bed.

Reluctantly, I would go upstairs and close my bedroom door. I would give it about five minutes before sneaking out and sitting on the top of the stairs to listen in to the grown-ups' conversation. The separation between adults and children was extreme back then and those few hours of forbidden eavesdropping were precious to me. Amazingly, I was never caught.

Used as I was to my loud father and his even louder (and drunken) brother, I was fascinated by this quiet man, Reginald - and it was always Reginald, never Reg or Reggie. His wife simply wouldn't allow it. He was the sort of man you could imagine coming out of the womb looking forty and with fully formed forty-something attitudes.

He was small, slim, unremarkable to look at, and always precisely dressed. Dapper was the expression they used back then. Although, curiously, it was the smaller men who were described in that way. Tall men were generally described as 'handsome'. And he was dapper right down to the razor-sharp parting in his Brylcreemed hair. For the dancing, like my father, he wore a black suit, white shirt and black bow tie. At work, I was told, he always wore either a three-piece grey suit or doubled-breasted blue pinstripe suit, white shirt, dark silk tie of red or blue, and highly polished black oxford shoes.

On the card nights, however, he would wear a herringbone Harris tweed sports jacket, grey flannel trousers and dark brown brogues. With a Viyella shirt and tweed tie. Always a tie, and always fastened tight in a single Windsor knot instead of the double knot he would wear for work. This was his version of the 'casual' look. Neither my father nor my uncle wore jackets and ties, and they always had their braces on show. All of which, of course, made Reginald look as formal as ever. But somehow still insignificant.

His wife, Irene, was even less significant. Quieter, mouse-like and subservient, only speaking when spoken to. Mrs meek and mild. She was shorter and slimmer than her husband, with an unmemorable face. A face that bore no makeup. Not even a trace of lipstick. Unlike my mother, a woman who never came downstairs in the morning without having applied full makeup and with her hair perfectly done. But Irene's meekness disappeared when she played cards. The golden rule in those days was that you didn't speak when a hand was being played and didn't criticise your partner or the other players in between hands. And friends playing together regularly adhered to that. Even when a few drinks had been taken. Rules were rules and weren't to be broken.

But not where Irene was concerned. The worm really turned when she had cards in her hand. She was a ferocious player who concentrated fully and never spoke, but often sighed loudly, shook her head and raised her eyebrows often when her husband played a card. And she was a *very* bad loser. The more gin and tonics she drank, the worse she became. In between hands, she would demand to know why someone had played such and such a card and how they had failed to understand her bidding. My mother, who was extremely tolerant (married to my father, she had to be) accepted Irene's behaviour, but my father did not. More than once he told Reginald to "control your bloody wife."

Reginald would just smile and say, "Lost cause, I'm afraid and I don't want to make my life a misery chasing that particular one. My life simply wouldn't be worth living." Which was a very odd thing for him to say given what I later learned about him.

Then, one Friday evening, they failed to appear, and my parents had to make do with a foursome at cards. The next one came around and still they weren't there. And from then on my parents had to call a taxi to take them into town. And that was it. I never saw either of them again.

I remember asking my mum why and she just brushed it aside saying, "no, we just don't see them anymore." In a tone I recognised even then. One that allowed no questions. I asked my brother – who was three years older than me – but he was none the wiser. And because they weren't of any real importance in my seven-year-old life, I simply forgot all about them.

It was years later, when I was seventeen and home from London where I was working, that the question of Reginald and Irene was raised again. I spotted a photograph on a table of them with my parents at a dance, and I asked my mum what had ever happened to them.

She thought about it for a while then finally told me the whole story. It was astonishing to me then, and still is whenever I think about it. Both in itself and because of the time when it happened: the middle fifties, those austere post-war years where nothing remarkable happened and the only scandals were those you read about in the News of The World. But this had been our very own, home-grown scandal.

Because Reginald was a nobody, really. An accountant. One of three partners in a decent little firm in the centre of town. His life, like his work I suppose, was a series of rigid routines. Every weekday morning was the same. His alarm was set for seven o'clock and he had shaved, dressed – in the clothes that his wife had laid out for him the previous night - and had his breakfast of bacon and eggs by eight.

Once finished he brushed his teeth, collected his briefcase and umbrella before kissing Irene goodbye. A single kiss, on the cheek, of course. He would then climb into his precious Rover saloon and set off for work, always arriving at half past eight. Except on the morning when he carried out all those routines… apart from one. Although he drove away from the house and was seen by the postman at the end of their street, he never arrived at the office.

Irene received a phone call from one of the other partners at 10 o'clock to ask where Reginald was.

"At work of course," she said. Surprised. "Why, is he not there? He should be there because he drove off at the usual time."

"That's why I'm calling," the partner said. He's not arrived, and that is so unusual, uniquely unusual, we wondered if he was ill, perhaps, or there was some domestic emergency or other?"

"No," she said, "not at all. He was perfectly fine. Everything was fine. And I haven't had a call from the police about any accident. I just don't understand."

"Yes. Neither do we," he said. "I will ensure that my secretary checks the hospitals. I will let you know the outcome. And do let us know if and when he turns up, won't you, and I will reciprocate."

The 'phone call ended, and Irene stood there for a long while, unable to deal with such an inexplicable break in routine. But she never was able to deal with it. Not ever. Because Reginald had vanished from the face of the earth. Never to be seen or heard from again. He had left no message and Irene never received any letters or postcards. Nor any birthday or Christmas cards.

Nothing. His car was never found, and in those days before modern camera coverage, there was no way of tracing his movements. And there was no evidence that he had gone abroad, either by car or on foot.

"The quiet ones are always the worst," my aunt said when she learned what had happened.

"Oh, that's a bit trite, Jen," my mum said. "That cliché's so old it's got hairs on it."

"It's true though," my aunt insisted. "The ones who keep on about how good they, are always the worst. And the ones who don't talk about themselves always have the deepest plans. And Gerald's turned out to be really deep. Who would have thought it? Nobody, that's who."

Three

Gerald's total disappearance would have been impossible today, of course. CCTV, traffic cameras and mobile 'phones would have combined to create a trail that was ridiculously easy to follow. But back then, to all intents and purposes, he had simply ceased to exist. Even now, some sixty years later, nothing has ever been discovered either about his whereabouts or whether he is still alive.

Although the police were contacted, they were not interested. A chap in his middle forties decides he's had enough of his marriage and work and does a disappearing act? Nothing too unusual in that and certainly nothing criminal. Little woman on the side, they assumed. No doubt one or two of the policemen who saw the report would have wished they could have done the same.

Irene found it impossible to understand. As did his firm. So much so that, after much discussion and, it must be said, great reluctance, the remaining two partners decided that they had to arrange for a forensic audit to be carried out. Annual audits of the firm had always been in place of course, but they had never unearthed any discrepancies whatsoever.

The truth is, though, that while small, theirs was an old-fashioned, long-established and highly regarded firm, so the pre-audit expectations were that everything would be in order. Also, the audits were carried out by men they knew from another firm in town, with the result that they found exactly what they expected to find. Everything was in order. Naturally. Chaps were chaps, not crooks. And this wasn't London.

Due to the peculiar circumstances, though, this particular audit was carried out by a firm from Manchester that specialised in forensic audits, especially where suspicion had arisen about a particular individual or group of individuals. They had no ties to any business community in our town and had no agenda other than to discover the hard, financial truth.

The results of their work dumbfounded everybody. The partners most of all. Because the investigations revealed that a total of £40,000 had disappeared from the firm's accounts. From Reginald's clients' accounts to be precise. This was an astonishing figure in 1955 when the average wage was fifteen pounds a week and a very decent house could be bought for £1,500. And it was a sum that would be worth well over a million pounds today.

Reginald had not stolen it all at once, of course, because even the casual annual audits would have uncovered that. Instead, they discovered that he had embezzled the money over an eight-year period since 1947, the year he had become a partner in the firm. Five thousand pounds a year he had siphoned money from the firm's clients and transferred it to…?

Because that was the question. Where had he placed the money, exactly? There was no evidence to show where it had gone. They could find no evidence of it in his personal bank account and a check with the other banks in town revealed no other accounts or safe-deposit boxes in his name.

His lifestyle hadn't changed at all: everything they owned and enjoyed fit perfectly with the salary that he earned. Their annual holiday in Scarborough was no extravagance and their house, their car and clothes also fit in with the money he both earned and spent. So where was it?

Despite the best efforts of the accountancy firm and the police - who had belatedly taken an interest - no trace of it was ever found.

The family joint account was healthy, showing only the usual regular, unchanging monthly deposits. The auditors recommended that it be reclaimed as part of the recompense, but the partners wouldn't hear of it. They were decent men, shocked at what had happened maybe, but they were not about to persecute a wife for the criminal activities of her husband. In fact, they were such decent men they even paid her the residue of his salary that was due. They did apologise however, for deeming that they considered it inappropriate to pay her a portion of his annual bonus.

But with the money she did receive, and the sale of their mortgage-free house, Irene was able to buy a small flat in town and live out the rest of her days in comfort. A desperate, lonely comfort it must be said, since they'd had no children, but comfortable at least. She even stopped going to church.

My mother said that she and a few other women friends tried to keep in touch and give her emotional support.

"I called on her just before she sold the house and asked her what I, what we, could do to help her. It wasn't what I wanted to do, I had no kind thoughts about her, but I made the offer."

"But why," I asked, "if you didn't like her."

"Because it was the right thing to do. Sometimes you do something, not because you want to, or you feel good about doing it, you do it just because it is the right thing to do. You'll learn that as you grow older. At least for your sake, I hope you will."

She was right, as my mother was in most things. I should have listened to her more in my teens. I would have turned out a better person.

"The offer was made," My mum continued, "but she rejected it. She said she'd lost the only thing that had really mattered to her. Lost the only man she'd ever truly loved. The fact that he'd left her without explanation, without reason, had devastated her. More so, she said, than if he'd divorced her, or he'd died. She could have rationalised the one and dealt with the other, she said, but she could never come to terms with what he'd actually done, especially the way in which he'd done it.

I was a little puzzled. "Because it was so brutal? Because it showed that he'd never really loved her?"

"Well... no not really," my mum said. It was mainly because her life had always been defined by Reginald's routines, his needs and wants, and now that they had disappeared along with him, she felt her life had no definition, direction, no certainties. She had lost all hope of having a better future. And she wasn't about to share her feelings about all that with anyone. Ever. Her rejection of us was so firm, so final, that we stopped trying. Eventually, we lost all contact with her, and she gradually disappeared from our conversations."

"That is so sad," I said. "Poor bloody woman. I can't imagine having such deep feelings about anybody."

My mother gave me one of her looks. Then smiled. "Of course not, because, nice as you are, you're still only a teenager. But it wasn't true, you see. She just adopted the behaviour she thought abandoned women should display. With heavy emphasis on the abandoned."

"Bit harsh mum," I said. "Why do you say that?"

"Because she didn't love him, not really. It was a mess, they were, her emotions I mean. I honestly think part of her was actually glad he'd disappeared. Because he was vile to her when they were together. Horrible. Nothing she ever did was right. Nothing pleased him and he wasn't shy about showing his feelings in front of others. Could be quite a nasty man, our

Reginald where she was concerned. Her behavior at cards was her little payback for the way he treated her."

"*Really*," I said, remembering the almost invisible little man I'd known as a child.

"Yes," she said. "You see, all of us women back in the fifties basically did what the men allowed us to. And it was no different whether you were a housewife or a movie star. It was just how it was back then. Especially husbands controlling their wives. But he took it to extreme lengths. She couldn't do anything, however small, without his permission."

"Then why did you spend time with him, the cards, the dancing?"

"Because your father and your uncles quite liked Reginald. He wasn't the same as them. Away from his wife he was quiet, reserved, a bit distant at times, never showing his emotions. But as often happens, opposites can attract. We wives accepted him because of her, even though none of us could ever get close to her. And anyway, we knew a little about why he behaved the way he did."

"How so," I asked, fascinated by now.

"Well, his parents were alcoholics, and as an only child he effectively brought himself up. He learned how to do everything for himself, everything practical that is, but because they never showed him any affection, any kindness, he never learned how to love. He never understood how to give love or recognise when it was being given, because he simply didn't know what it was. And if you don't learn to recognise love, what it means to be loved when you're very young it's almost impossible to learn it in later life."

"Really?" I asked. "What, never?"

"No," she said. "Not unless you meet someone remarkable who can help you discover what love and kindness are. Which he never did. And because he didn't understand what they were, didn't understand goodness, he wasn't able to realise that he was bad. He ended up scarred inside, and internal scars almost never heal. We knew it wasn't really his fault, so we tolerated him because of that."

"Blimey," I said. "I never knew my mum was such a philosopher."

She laughed. "I wouldn't go that far. But by the time you've reached my age, you do tend to have learned a thing or two about relationships."

"Especially when married to dad?"

"Now, now, that's quite enough of that, young man. Behave yourself."

But she hadn't denied it.

And that was the last time we ever talked about the 'scandal'.

As for Reginald, no one ever did discover where the money had gone, or where he had disappeared to. And the crime never made the newspapers. Yes, there was a small piece in the local rag about his disappearance, but of the crime and the amount of money involved, there was no mention. Something else that would have been impossible in this day and age. The national press would have picked it up, plus the story would have gone viral on social media. There would have been no hiding place at all.

Had he gone abroad perhaps? Something that was ridiculously easy in those simpler, more innocent days. Drive to a port, buy your ticket and drive onto the ferry. No need to show a passport in most cases. And since he must have assumed that he was now a wanted man – albeit a comparatively low-priority, white-collar criminal - it would have been the logical choice. Was he on his own? With another woman? Possible, but unlikely I thought.

It is said that the only motives for serious crimes are love or money. Well, Reginald certainly had the money, but had he also found love as well? Did he have a woman he'd somehow managed to keep in secret for years? Perhaps. But I'd hate to think he found another woman to mistreat as he did Irene.

Or, worse, that he'd found one who showed him how to love and be loved. A woman who helped him understand what love was. I sometimes imagined him living in France, perhaps, Spain or Holland even, having enjoyed a second life in the company of a woman who loved him. But I sincerely hoped not.

Because the quiet man did not deserve that at all.

We sat on a bench in St James Park. Wasted and wounded, as Tom Waits once sang. Slumped, side by side as the ducks and pigeons waddled hopefully around our feet. Sorry guys, no bread tonight.

Wasted because of the amount of Youngs bitter and Jamesons we'd taken on board during a four-hour session after work. And wounded because of a disagreement with some customers in the Buckingham Arms on Petty France. Which was in part a soldiers' pub thanks to the Horse Guards barracks just across the road. But soldiers were always in the minority and because it was so close to their barracks, they didn't cause any trouble. As a rule.

And there hadn't been any tonight, wouldn't have been, not until Matt spotted a couple of civilians with their women. And took an instant, irrational, dislike to what appeared to be a normal foursome. Doing no-one any harm, doing nothing to offend. Just drinking and chatting, with lots of smiles and some laughter. The men were suited and booted fit looking guys, one tall and dark, the other much shorter and pink-cheeked. The two women with them were polar opposites though. One was the sort of woman who would turn heads, women as well as men, and create unfulfilled dreams in most men.

The other, though, could best be described as homely. As in Battersea Dogs Home, homely, Matt said. Loudly. Staring directly at them. While his free hand twitched constantly, and the redness crept slowly up his neck. Should I have spotted the familiar signs and moved us out there and then? Well of course I should. On another day I might well have done. Ah, but an excess of alcohol blurs the judgement and makes fools of us all.

Matt took our empty pint glasses and targeted the foursome as he shouldered his way to the bar. I downed my Jameson – wasn't going to waste that, whatever happened – and stepped closer to the group as Homely Woman turned to Matt and glared.

"Excuse me!" she said, as she started wiping the spilled drink from her jacket.

"Bloody hell," Matt said. "That's a surprise."

"What is?" she asked.

"It speaks," Matt replied.

"Yes? And?"

"It speaks English."

"So? Your point being?"

"Well, you're so bleedin' ugly, darlin', I thought you'd just bark like the dog you are."

Pink-cheek didn't say a word. Just turned and slammed Matt full on the nose with the heel of his hand. I heard the crunch and saw the blood as his mate threw a punch at me. I turned my head, but not quickly enough. He caught the corner of my eye above my cheekbone and sent me staggering back against a table.

He kept on coming as I saw Matt being punched in the face. I went to knee the guy between the legs but hit his thigh before his balls. That made him stop for a second, but he didn't double over or drop to his knees. He was still in the game. I was scrabbling for a glass to finish it when

I spotted five others getting up at the back of the pub. They moved towards us, clearly intending some serious harm. The haircuts said squaddies and my heart sank. I suddenly realised these first two must be officers. The slightly longer hair disguising them as civilians. Matt had a bar stool in both hands, while I was holding a pint glass and an empty bottle. But I knew we were in for a severe beating.

Luckily, the officers weren't really up for it. Not wanting to mess on their own doorstep I expect. They held their hands up to the five who had just made their way through the crowd and shook their heads.

It still could have been mayhem because Matt was threatening them with the stool like an old-fashioned lion tamer. I managed to grab his arm as two of the staff came over the bar. Between us, we hustled Matt out into the street.

We walked off as quickly as we could. When we looked back the barmen were still there on the pavement outside watching us. So we ducked around the corner and crossed into the park to catch our breath. And assess the damage. I had a deep cut next to my eye. A boxer's cut most likely caused by the ring the guy was wearing. Using my handkerchief and Matt's newspaper, though, I eventually managed to stop the bleeding. Matt was in a much worse state. He sat on the bench, his head between his knees, as the blood from his ruined nose dripped steadily onto the path. Part of me said just leave him and head off home before the night got any worse, but the better part said stay.

Because although he wasn't a close friend – this was only the third or fourth time I been out drinking with him in the two years we'd worked together - he was a good colleague, one who'd helped me on several occasions without being asked. Despite his comparative youth – we were both twenty-six - he was far and away the best political analyst in the company. With my youthful arrogance, I thought I had a decent brain, proven by my Economics degree from Bristol. But it didn't take me long to realise I was strictly average compared to Matt with his First in PPE from the London School of Economics and an intellect to match.

He was respected in the company for his qualities and in two short years had become head of the political analysis unit. But he wasn't well liked. Too arrogant, too aggressive, and too confrontational for people to warm to him. He was always ready for a verbal battle and scathingly dismissive of those who either didn't agree with him or simply couldn't grasp his analyses and arguments. The phrase "Doesn't suffer fools gladly", could have been coined just for him.

Me? I quickly learned when to keep my mouth shut when he was off on one, especially in meetings.

He was a man of strange contradictions. He had his suits made to measure by a Savile Row tailor and he wore hand-made shoes from Lobbs of St James's. From that, his looks, intellect, manner and professionalism, you would have said he was solid middle class. Probably public school educated. Until he opened his mouth that is. Then his raw London accent told a very different story. His attitude and aggression only added to the confusion. It was only when we had an extended pub lunch one day that I learned some of the reasons why. I asked him where he lived, thinking that, like me, he'd be sharing a house or flat with some other young professionals. In Kennington, Islington, one of those areas.

"I live in a council flat in Pimlico," he'd said. "Just me and my old man. Mum passed a couple of years ago, cancer, so it's just me and him. Ex-boxer. And not a very good one."

"You get on well with him then," I said, "seeing as you still live with him."

"Not at all," he said. "He's a fascist pig. A pure thug. When I was growing up, anything he saw as disobedience, insolence, whatever, wasn't with met with reason or debate but by outright physical violence. Didn't take me long to realise his intellectual limits were too small to be measured."

"You didn't get your brains from him, then, Matt."

"Christ no. I got them all from mum. Bright, intelligent woman she was. Really bright, but the most she ever did was get a job as classroom assistant at the local Primary."

"So what happened," I asked, intrigued.

"The 1950s, that's what happened, my friend. Working-class girls didn't get an education back then. Had to leave school even earlier than the boys. She'd been born into a different family, or different time, she'd have matched anybody, could easily've been anything she wanted. The waste in that generation's nothing short of criminal."

"So she was the one who helped you?"

"Absolutely. She'd tell me again and again that the only way to escape, to get away from my old man was through education, education, education. It was her mantra. And she was right. One teacher at school, Mrs Davies, she had almost as much faith in me as my mum did, and then the LSE was the making of me, as the elders say. But I'd never have done it if she hadn't spent hour after hour helping me with my homework. She understood stuff way quicker than me but had this incredible way of explaining it so simply in a way I could understand. Gotta say, better than a lot of the lecturers at LSE. But then she didn't have their arrogance. Up their own arses don't come near some of them."

"But somehow you've got stuck here with him," I said.

"Yeah. Laziness on my part I suppose. Staying there after she died was always the easy option. Cuts the independence a bit but gives me a lot more money in my pocket. And the intelligence I inherited from her helps me deal with the violence I learned from him. But both sides are always there. I just have to maintain the balance. Which I can do, most of the time…"

"Except when you're drunk."

"You got it Mark. Alcohol always tips the scales. And always the wrong way. Work is the one place where I can keep it in check. Instead of punching some guys, which I'm very tempted to do at times, I just destroy them with words instead."

We'd never talked about anything as personal since that day, and I thought about it as I sat next to him on the bench.

"You need to get that seen to, Matt" I said, pointing to his nose. "Where's the nearest hospital?"

"Hospital? In this condition? Oh yeah, they just love guys walking into A&E late at night, pissed out of their brains, blood everywhere. No way they'd do a proper job. No, we'll go to my place. The old man'll sort it out. When he couldn't fight any more, he became a corner-man. Knows all the tricks."

We cleaned up his face as best we could, but it still took a while before any taxi driver would agree to take us to Pimlico. His father was in the kitchen clearing up before he went to bed. A short, stocky man bearing the flattened nose and eyebrow scars of an old boxer. He looked me up and down.

"Who's this then," he asked Matt.

"Just a mate from work," Matt replied.

"Another clever bastard are you?" he said looking hard at me. "Ever done a proper day's work in your life, 'ave you?"

I just shrugged and raised my eyebrows. Couldn't think of anything useful to say to that.

"Well, you weren't so bleedin' clever tonight, were you, judging by the state of you both."

He shook his head, dragged over a kitchen chair and sat Matt down next to the sink. He soaked a flannel under the hot tap and used it to clean off all the dried blood on Matt's nose and cheeks.

"Hold 'is 'ead steady," he said to me when he'd finished. Then he took Matt's nose in both hands and with a sharp twisting, tugging, pushing motion, put it back into something like its old shape and form. A final squeeze with forefinger and thumb and he was done. Although his face had gone white, Matt was completely silent through the whole procedure.

"Pack it with cotton wool and take a coupla aspirin 'fore you kip down," he said. "You'll 'ave a right pair of shiners in the mornin' but otherwise you'll be as right as rain. And no more bleedin' alcohol, right?"

Then, to my surprise, he turned to me, cleaned my cut, and dabbed on some antiseptic before covering it with some evil-smelling greasy stuff he got from a battered old green tin. Nodded at me and took himself off to bed.

"Not very sociable is he," I said once he was safely upstairs.

"That *was* him being sociable," Matt said. "For some weird reason he seemed to like you and that's unusual."

"Really?"

"Yeah. Look, he spoke to you, which is rare, and then he cleaned and fixed your cut without either of us asking. And that's more than rare, I can tell you. In fact if I hadn't seen it myself, I wouldn't have believed it."

I absorbed this information while Matt and I brewed up and took our cuppas and biscuits into the front room. I stopped and stared then commented on the BNP posters in the front window.

"My old man," he said. "Told you he was a thug. Real fascist bastard he is. Mum kept him on a tight rein but since she died, he's been full-on."

He nodded over to one wall. "Check out the shelves and you'll see what I mean. He's a member of some very dodgy book clubs."

I stood and examined the two rows of books. Biographies of Hitler and other prominent Nazis together with a random collection of Nazi and Second World War histories and quite a few of those 'true-life' novels by ex-SAS soldiers. More disturbing were the books about race theory and the deficiencies of the negro brain. I shook my head as I turned to him.

"You didn't follow in his footsteps, then, Matt?"

"You must be bloody joking. You ever spent any time with these skinheads? Thick as shit, they are. Except not the leaders so much. Nasty, clever bastards some of them, but they only use their cleverness to control the braindeads. Bit like training dogs. They'd be better off training them for Walthamstow track."

I laughed.

"I'm not joking. Seriously, if that lot and their type keep on breeding the way they do, there'll be no hope left for us."

"Us in England, you mean?"

"No, Mark, the whole of mankind."

ONE MORE CUP OF COFFEE

The tall, elderly, man sat outside a café-bar in Covent Garden. It was a beautiful Indian Summer evening and the pavements swarmed with people seeking food and drink. The man had taken one of four chairs at a table, but no-one detached themselves from the crowds to enquire whether any were free. This was partly due to him having placed his suit jacket over the back of one of the chairs and set his briefcase down on another. But it was also due to the man himself. There was something about him, something indefinable, but real, that prevented people from approaching him.

The waiter brought him his coffee and brandy and five minutes later a younger, dark-haired, man slid into the seat opposite. He placed his cigarettes, lighter and phone on the table. The tall man smiled and nodded an acknowledgement.

"Well hello, Patrick. Still smoking those disgusting French cigarettes, I see."

"I like strong flavours in all things, David. As well you should know."

He pushed his sunglasses down to the end of his nose and stared across the table. The face was the same, gaunt and pale, with that patrician nose. And a full head of white hair. Which was surprising, since he must be at least eighty years old. The older man stared back and raised his eyebrows.

"Yes, Patrick?"

"Just checking, David. It must be ten years since we last met. I was just making sure it was you."

"Interesting," the tall man said. "I had to do a double take when I first saw you because you are dressed very casually, if I may say so."

"It may have escaped your notice, David, but you are almost certainly the only person in the whole of Covent Garden who is wearing a suit. A very nice linen, summer suit it must be said, but a suit, nonetheless. And a collar and tie – both of which remain fastened."

The tall man grimaced. "That is quite possibly the case, but I have never quite understood why a few hours of sunshine should cause one to lower one's standards."

Patrick laughed. "Yes, I could well imagine you wearing a suit, shirt and tie in India during the Raj."

"I did." A statement which completely stopped the conversation until the tall man asked a question.

"So why are you without jacket, young Patrick?"

"Because I dropped it into a waste bin along with a tweed cap not twenty minutes ago after I finished my last job. Wore them before and during, got rid of them afterwards and put my sunglasses on. In a crowded London that is quite sufficient to completely change one's appearance."

The tall man raised his eyebrows. "A job? One of ours?"

"Of course, David. Who else would I be working for?"

"Forgive me, but after the last one, I thought we were taking pause."

"But you gave me two at once, David, remember?"

The tall man waved an airy hand as if to say the actual allocation of unpleasant tasks was quite beneath him.

"And exactly what is it that you've just completed for us?"

"The Westminster councillor who's been making waves? I quietly despatched him as he watched a film in the Leicester Square cinema."

The tall man stared at him, eyebrows raised. "A cinema? A public place on a Sunday afternoon? Have you taken leave of your senses?"

"You forget how long I have been doing this, David. I used subtlety. At my age I find I have to find subtler, less strenuous, ways of working."

"Pray tell."

"You're interested? Really?" Patrick asked, not believing it for a moment and wondering what the man's motive was.

"Of course. I am always interested in techniques and methodology. The way you chaps operate is a complete mystery to me."

"Very well. For this one, I used a spoke from a motorbike wheel, shortened and then sharpened to a needle point. I wandered in behind the target, sat next to him and, at an appropriate time, I simply inserted it between his ribs and into his heart. There was no blood and no unnatural physical reaction. Just a man sitting forward a little and then resting back. If anyone did see him move, they would simply assume he was laughing along with everyone else."

The tall man didn't respond, simply signalled to the waiter and pointed a finger hand to indicate the same for himself.

"And what is your pleasure Patrick?"

Patrick turned and spoke directly to the waiter. "A pint of Guinness and a large Jamesons please. The 18-year-old if you have it. Thank you."

"Not lost your plebeian tastes, I see young Patrick."

Patrick laughed. "Plebian? Not at all. The black nectar is the drink of kings and princes. As well as all my Irish forebears. And there's nothing in the least plebeian about the 18-year-old Jamesons, David, one of the finest Whiskeys around. Speaking of plebs, I notice you still don't address the servant class directly unless you absolutely must. Hand signals are quite sufficient for the lower orders, eh?"

"I find it quite sufficient to communicate one's wishes, thank you."

You insufferable, pompous old goat, Patrick thought. How was I ever taken in by you back then? Youth, I suppose. Callow youth. Coupled with unforgivable ambition. Please God do not let him start with the reminiscences. Let's give him a poke.

"For my part, David," he said, I cannot remember when I last spoke to someone who wasn't serving me food or drink, driving me in their cab, or delivering parcels to my home. Without your plebs, I'd have absolutely no-one to talk to."

The older man didn't react.

"And since we're speaking about the subject of communication, David, I must say I am curious. Why are we meeting face to face after all this time? You are usually so fanatical about observing the cut-out protocol."

"I simply wanted to see you again, Patrick. It has been such a long time and I wondered how you were. I always remember you as my first recruit. A young officer, fresh out of the forces

– special forces, as I recall – and a perfect mix of intelligence and brutality, coupled with sublime manners. A middle-class thug of the best kind. In other words, a perfect example of the required operative."

Lord save us all from an old man's horseshit, Patrick thought. And his sentimental memories. But I just knew he would indulge himself.

"But how am I David? Physically fine, as you can see. Regular walking and swimming keep me in shape. So much so I can still fit into my old uniform. Sadly, worn only at funerals these days. Mentally, well that's another matter…" He waited until the waiter had delivered their drinks and accepted the ten-pound note David offered. An acceptable tip to ensure decent service amongst the chaos, David explained.

"As I was saying… mentally? Well, I find myself subject to increasing bouts of introspection and reflection on the life I have led. And I do not understand why. Perhaps it is simply a matter of accumulation. There may be, after all, a limit to God's forgiveness. Possibly it is the case that once the number of our sins reaches a certain level, they simply become unacceptable to Him. Does He then withdraw the protection of His forgiveness and leave the mind to deal with one's actions over the years?"

He paused for a moment and lit a cigarette. "Or perhaps it is simply my age. At 62, I have a lot less time left on this earth than I have already spent walking upon it. The future is opaque and very uncertain compared to my past."

He drank half of his Jamesons and then followed it with a healthy mouthful or two of Guinness. Wondering if he had revealed too much. Honesty wasn't welcomed, or respected, in this business. Always regarded as weakness.

"Forgive me for saying so, Patrick, but you almost sound as if you're approaching your end days."

"Oh, I do hope not, David. I'd like to think that you'd be my last. That I would be asked to despatch you as my final, grand gesture, the curtain call on my career. "This one and no more," is what I'd like to say."

The older man smiled and shook his head. "But that absolutely will not happen. You do realise that, I trust. My retirement will be spent happily walking and gardening in my beloved Cotswolds. Cricket and roses and fine wine will see me through well enough."

"Yes, David. I know. So, I'll just keep on doing this until you, they, have no further use for me. And then they will of course, kill me in return. I have no illusions. I'm expendable, I know, I have always known it, so it really doesn't matter."

"Doesn't matter? Oh, come now Patrick, of course it does. What is it they say? If one death matters, then surely every single one does."

Patrick shook his head. "Ah, that is too trite, David. You see, it's my belief that a person's death only matters to those left behind who will genuinely miss them. Those who loved them… or simply liked them, perhaps. That's where the impact is, where it matters. It goes no further than that. Isn't that so?"

"Yes, if you put it like that, Patrick, I suppose so. But then everybody has someone who will miss them. Someone who will mourn their loss. Even momentarily."

Patrick shook his head again.

"The truth is there's no-one for me, David. No-one will be affected in the slightest when I go. No-one to grieve, no-one to mourn. No-one to miss me at all. Just someone to dispassionately close the book and remove me from the active list. A simply matter of bureaucracy. But I've had a damned good run - longer than I could ever have expected. So, as I say, it doesn't really matter, does it?"

"Perhaps not. But what does matter is your recent performance."

Ah, Patrick thought, that is what today is all about, is it? A question of me being disciplined? A metaphorical smack on the wrist for the naughty boy? Well, let's not make it too easy, eh? I never did so for the school prefects or my senior officers, and I'm certainly not about to start now.

"My last one went off without a hitch, David. As I have just described."

"I was referring to the previous task, as you well know. That did not go well."

"Perhaps so. But no-one told me the subject would have his young son with him. No-one told me he had a child in the first place. I can hardly be blamed for someone else's poor research and briefing, now, can I? And for you information, I do not kill six-year-old children."

"That may well be the case, Patrick, but I have to say the clients were unhappy at the outcome. Very unhappy indeed. As was I, for that matter. I had to return the fee and I do not enjoy doing that. It's not the money, it's the principle."

"Ah, 'the principle', is it? Then you should have no difficulty understanding that I do not kill children – on principle."

"Hang your bloody principles, Patrick. The clients expected anyone else to be dealt with if the situation arose. I do not consider that to be an unreasonable expectation on their part."

Patrick took another mouthful of Guinness while he considered how to respond.

"Well," he said eventually, "had they told me, briefed me properly, then I would have found a way to remove the parent when the child wasn't around. It's very simple to do so. And they said there was no particular urgency. So I used my judgement and walked away ready to do it another time. But then you called me off. And gave it to someone else - if the evening news is to be believed. And the child was killed."

The older man finished his brandy and waited until Patrick lit another cigarette before he spoke again.

"Has it ever crossed your mind that the subject kept the child very close because he knew what was going to happen to him? That perhaps he imagined it would afford him some protection."

"That is totally beside the point, David. Assumptions about me should not have been made. After all, there would have been times when the child was not there, or asleep, and I could have easily completed the job."

"It's odd, but I have never known you have such scruples before, Patrick."

"Oh, I have always had them, David. You just never caused me to pay attention to them before."

The older man considered him for a moment and then he nodded slightly to acknowledge the point. "Hmmm, perhaps you are right. But are there any other scruples we should know about? Ancient or modern?" He paused. "Women, perhaps? The disabled? What other lines have you drawn that I am unaware of."

"None that I can think of David. You have already had me kill women and old people both. As for disabled, I clearly remember the man in a wheelchair - if that counts. But I do not kill children."

"May I ask why?"

"I don't know, David. Something in my upbringing perhaps? I was one once, you know. A child." He laughed.

The tall man stiffened, and something changed in his eyes as he leaned forward across the table. But he didn't laugh.

"Humour is a poor weapon to use at this particular juncture, Patrick. And though you have attempted to deflect, I'm still curious about your aversion to killing children."

Patrick didn't respond immediately while he again considered what to say. This was new territory for him because past conversations with the older man had always been about business, never personal. He had no idea if the man was married, even. And they had never discussed feelings. He thought for a while and then simply decided to be honest. For once. Be interesting to see where it leads.

"Very well. What it is, I believe the sins of their elders have nothing at all to do with any children involved. They are, quite literally, innocent in these affairs and are not deserving of punishment or harm."

"But what about a life without a parent?" the tall man asked. "One or both. Surely that is harmful to a child? Might it not, perhaps, cause a lifetime of harm? Most especially if the child sees the parent killed in front of them."

Patrick shook his head and finished his Whiskey before he spoke.

"Children can, and often do, recover from trauma. Whereas there can be absolutely no recovery from death."

"Hmmm. And you accused me of being trite. Those are not considerations that can be entertained in our line of work, Patrick. The fact that you do worries me, quite frankly."

"But now that you know of them, David, you simply make some slight adjustments, surely?"

The older man smiled. "Yes, I am sure some suitable adjustments can be made in order to accommodate your wishes, Patrick. Since you are our longest serving operative, I'm sure they can be. But for now, our cups and glasses are empty. Indulge an old man, won't you, and join me in a coffee and brandy."

He signalled the waiter again and ordered two espressos and large brandies. Patrick turned to the waiter.

"No brandy for me thanks. Just a coffee and another large Jamesons please."

Neither man spoke again until the waiter had delivered the drinks. The older man raised his coffee cup in a toast.

"To us, Patrick, and our mutually profitable relationship in the service of our country."

Both men drained their espressos and sat back. Patrick lit another cigarette. And then realised he couldn't feel it between his lips. Or between his fingers. It fell to the floor between his feet, but he found that he couldn't bend forward to pick it up. And the realisation suddenly struck him.

The coffee! You idiot! The waiter is one of David's. Christ! Stupid, stupid, stupid. Too old, too slow and too bloody smug. He went to lift his hand and point at Patrick across the table but found he couldn't move it. Tears seeped from his eyes. He began to speak but his voice sounded bizarre and his tongue felt sticky and thick. But he did manage to get the words out.

"I hope whatever you had put in my coffee isn't what I think it is, David."

"Hope? Hopes are nothing more than dreams that we carry with us, Patrick. But dreams don't help one cope with reality, do they? And after all, when hope dies, what is there left to dream about." Then he smiled and gently shook his head.

"Don't worry, it is quite painless and quick, dear boy, or so they tell me. And quite undetectable. All the signs of a heart attack apparently. See you on the other side, Patrick. Bye now."

Patrick found that he couldn't even move his eyes to follow the older man and he quickly disappeared from his vision. His last thought - and final regret - was that while he had drained his coffee cup, he hadn't finished his Jameson.

CHAS

One

Chas was around. Chas was always around. Or "abaht", as they said in his part of London. "Chas abaht?" Someone would ask and receive the appropriate reply.

A man who was often seen, but never really noticed. Five feet and a bit of instantly forgettable human being. A dapper little chap, though, who was always dressed well. Better than smart. But the saying, "clothes maketh the man" didn't apply to him. People noticed the clothes immediately and remembered them but forgot him in no time at all.

They remembered his clothes because he was real old-school with it. A man who understood the value of dressing with style, precision and cohesion. Didn't care about his peers, whatever the fashion of the day might be. For him it was all nineteen sixties style like his dad and uncles. Saw the old photographs and loved the look. Crombie overcoats, mohair suits, tab-collar shirts, silk ties and scarves, American brogues, and hi-shine loafers. Scoured London and the internet searching for the right stuff. As a result, he looked good, authentic, but out of his time, really.

He was almost invisible though, because all anybody ever remembered about him apart from the clothes was his lack of height. Those people who saw him for the first time? That was it. All of it. Hey, who's the little guy?

And witnesses? Well, they just couldn't cope. "Oh yeah, there was another guy there… really little guy… I mean really tiny… No, normal looking otherwise... sorry Officer, what can I tell you?"

Which made him useful of course. Especially for the cash pick-ups. And we are talking serious cash. He could glide through crowds, out of sight, without bending or dipping the knees. Never too quick, never too slow. No change of pace to draw the watchers' eyes. He'd slip in unnoticed, load up the wheelie suitcase, business done, and gone before the coppers even realized he was there. Hopped a bus and was gone. Off into a different manor in minutes.

No ducking and diving when he left, either. Just strolled right past them. Because who notices a wheelie suitcase in London these days? Nobody. So no worries about being collared, not when they hadn't the first clue who or what they were even looking for. Because apart from his lack of height, Chas had a collection of reversible coats and a few different hats, caps and glasses. Transformation took less than five seconds.

And when he wore the school uniform with blazer and shorts - taking the absolute piss, AC/DC style - he became totally invisible. Yes, the presence of a schoolboy might be spotted, caught on CCTV even, but always dismissed out of hand. Schoolboy, early teens? Involved in serious drug-related naughties? Never considered. Never remembered. Never linked. But he hadn't always been trusted to pick up the cash. Not at all. Seen as a risk at first.

"Not sure who to put in tomorrow, boss."

"What about that new kid I've seen around. What's his name?"

"Chas."

"Chas? What? That it?"

"Says that's all that's needed."

"Huh."

"And he's not a kid, he's twenty-five. He's just short is all."

"Short? He's almost bleedin' non-existent. Point is, he any good?"

"We'll find out soon enough. Think I'll have to stick him in tomorrow anyway, 'cos most of our other faces are too well known now. And the old bill will be hard pushed to spot him in a crowd."

"But is he up for it? Can he handle himself alright?"

"Oh yeah. He was Col's mate – remember Col? Reckoned this mate of his was sound. Been doing the arcades since we took him on. Col was right. Reliable sort. Just gets on with it. No fuss. And despite his size, never takes a backward step. Got some bottle. Be fine I reckon."

They put it to him and he was well keen. Almost too keen. Should they, shouldn't they? In the end lack of other safe bodies tipped it. So they gave him the suitcase, the directions, and put him in. And waited. Sure enough, it went off without a hitch. Smooth as. Same with the next three or four. Not a ripple. He became known as "The Collector" from thereon in. Or "The Ghost" as some called him.

And so they used him, but they didn't know him. Nobody did. He was just a functioning part of the operation, not a person. Oh, they knew he was local. Because of his accent, which placed him somewhere in the vicinity of the Old Kent or Walworth Roads. But no actual address because whenever people asked him in the early days – and that wasn't often – he would just say he lived local. He said that because he was still living with his Mum - at his age. And you don't tell people that when you're trying to be jack the lad. I mean. Stands to reason.

The thing was if people asked him once, about anything, they never asked a second time. They just weren't interested enough. They didn't not like him, you understand, they just didn't know, and didn't really care, who he was.

Two

There was the girl who answered the phone for the Wholesale Stationary company – the legitimate front for the business. She liked him well enough, liked the look of him. And he'd chat to her in the mornings when he came in to make his coffee. About TV, music, clothes and stuff. Easy to chat to. And he always had that look in his eyes as well. Like he knew something no-one else did. Or could. What it was? She never asked and he never said.

Sometimes he'd bring her a decent coffee from Starbucks instead of the instant rubbish they had in the office. Even brought her a blueberry muffin once in a while. She said he shouldn't 'cos it would make her fat. He just laughed. They both knew she could eat three or four of those a day and never put on an ounce.

But the first time she realised he was different, was when the flowers appeared on her desk. Flowers? Dandelions and daisies, they were. Huh. She wasn't too impressed.

"These down to you?" she asked when he walked into her office later that day.

"Yeah, thought you might like some flowers to brighten the place up."

She gave him a look. "But they're not flowers, are they? They're just weeds."

"Nooo, you shouldn't say that, call them weeds. Just because somebody years ago stuck that label on them, doesn't mean you have to. Because they're still flowers. Local. Grown in this manor. You know that empty plot by the filling station? Well that's where I picked them. So they're proper, they are, our flowers, not some over-cultivated things from abroad - Holland or wherever. So please don't disrespect them. And anyway, what happened to 'it's the thought that counts'?"

"Weren't too much of a thought, that's what," she said.

He laughed, a nice laugh, then turned and left. She shook her head and swung around back to her screen. Weird or what, she thought.

Then one day he asked her why she was working there.

"Why not," she said, "it's a job like any other."

"Not exactly though is it," he said. "They're very questionable people to say the least. And you must know it."

She ignored that. "So why are you working here, in that case?" she asked.

"Because I'm a bad lad. It fits me. But you're not like me, you're a good girl, I can tell. So I was wondering how you got to know them in the first place?"

"My dad and his brothers have worked for them before."

He just said "Aaah", nodded his head slowly and never mentioned it again. But he did ask her a strange question another day. Asked her if she ever felt like leaving it all behind and go off travelling.

"Not with any specific destination in mind, but just to get away. And keep on travelling until something happened to make you stop. And stay there, knowing nothing and nobody. You ever feel like that?"

"No I bleedin' don't," she said. "Never. And I gotta tell you, nobody else has ever asked me anything like that before." She cocked her head to one side and looked at him. "You're a deep one and no mistake, ain't you?"

He was quiet for a while then said, "Well just don't stay too long, that's all. Don't stay until you find you want to leave but can't. I know it was drummed into us as kids that the grown-ups always know what's best for us, but the fact is they don't. Because they don't know, and don't care, what we want for ourselves. So be careful is all I'm saying."

Then he walked out of her little office and never raised the subject again.

She tested him one afternoon, though. Because nobody knew anything about him, she asked him who he was.

"I don't know who or what I am," he said. "Certainly not enough to explain it to myself, never mind anybody else. I've got this far in life accepting too much and questioning too little. It's a bit like walking in a thick fog. You know you're moving but you don't know where you are or where you're going. You keep hoping to bump into a lamp post to give yourself a solid reference point. I've never hit my lamp post."

She stared at him like he had two heads but only three eyes. She thought about his answer many times but couldn't begin to understand what he'd been going on about. She never questioned him again.

But he never failed to put his head round the door to say goodnight when he left. Nice. Did this little thing where it looked like he was tipping a hat to her. She told him it looked old-fashioned, and he said he'd seen his granddad do it for real and thought it looked cool – stylish even.

When she thought about it, she found herself agreeing with him. That little gesture, moving two fingers and a thumb onto an imaginary hat brim while he dipped his head, well that did look kind of stylish.

But there was no question of anything developing with him she told her friend 'Chelle in the pub one night. He weren't tall enough. Simple as that.

"Yeah, I like him well enough, he's polite, respectful, but I can't go out with a guy who's six inches shorter than me, now can I? Look like I was taking me little brother down the shops. Not natural, is it? Can't be seen out with a short arse, can you? Never live it down round 'ere."

"But he's real good looking though."

"I know, I know. But that's no good when he's nowhere near my size, is it? If only he was a foot taller, then you'd be talking, 'Chelle."

Michelle laughed. "Here," she said, "d'you reckon he's the same size all over? I mean, you know, his prick."

"Your mind! Honestly 'Chelle. And no he's normal down there, nothing tiny about it."

"Oh yes," Michelle said. "And how would you know that then?"

"If you must know, I'm a crotch-watcher, arn' I?" she said, blushing. "There was a decent sized bulge last time I looked. No, it's just his height. Way too short."

"There are better reasons for not liking somebody you know."

"Well that one's mine and it's the only one I got. Don't need another one. And I don't not like him, because I do actually, it's just he's too short for me. Okay?"

"Yeah, I suppose."

"Oh come off it, 'Chelle. You suppose? Seriously, can you imagine me taking him home? My dad would destroy him. And as for me brothers, well…"

"Your Mum'd like him."

"She don't count compared to the others. I couldn't, no way."

"Okay, I get it. It's a shame though. Because he looks well tasty, way he dresses."

"Oh yeah. But that's only 'cos he's so small he has to have everything tailor made. Suits, shirts, jeans, shoes, the lot. Spends an absolute fortune on his gear."

And thereby dismissed what was quite possibly the best thing about him. Apart from his personality, that is. But she still noticed him. Mainly for the way he dressed, you understand.

Three

Then one morning she didn't see him in the place. After a couple of days, she realised he simply wasn't around anymore. Chas wasn't abaht no more. Anywhere. And nobody was talking about him. And she thought it better not to ask. It struck her that she missed him. Surprised herself. Even though there was nothing going on between them she found she liked the place much better when he was around. Niceness makes a difference she thought. Yes.

He'd been there the evening before, saying goodnight on his way home, but no sign of him since. And a new guy, another shorty, was there in his place. Looking like he belonged already. Tried to chat to her as well but she weren't having none of that. As if. Bleedin' cheek on 'im. She heard the word "skimming", later that day. Just an echo really, but it was enough to make her stop and think. Had he skimmed, she wondered? Skimmed too much, maybe? Because it was understood that everybody did it. Just had to keep it sensible, is all. Within limits. Whatever the limits were. Second thoughts, and worse, maybe he'd been skimming off the wrong people?

And had they...?

No. She killed that thought before it could grow. She had no way of knowing what they might or might not have done to him. Because these were very naughty chaps, she'd come to understand that. Privately though, she hoped they hadn't. Hoped and prayed he'd seen the signs and had it away on his toes.

And then sat quietly for a long while, thinking about what he'd said about getting stuck. About not being able to get out if she wanted to. And thinking about where he might be. But then apart from the top couple of guys, nobody knew. And nobody dared ask them. To be honest? Nobody cared that much. Not about Chas. Why would you?

Because he was just this really little guy who was always around. But wasn't any more. Nothing else to say about it, really.

Fat Albert was confused. He was called Fat Albert because, well, that's what he was. Fat. And tall. Six feet five inches tall, although the fat he carried made him look shorter. The twenty-four stones of fat he had carried for over fifty years, managing a questionable boozer in Stepney. And managing it very successfully too. Until his knees gave out. Since he was a man who'd worked for an equally questionable firm for over thirty years, knew what the score was and always kept his mouth shut, he was given the job of looking after things at the warehouse.

His sister marrying the guv'nor hadn't done any harm either of course. Now, instead of the constant minor hassles in the pub, he could sit all day smoking, frinking the occasional beer, eating the delicious sandwiches his Dor' had prepared for him - and watching internet porn.

"But straight, mind you," he always told people who questioned his habit. "I don't watch nothing depraved, no kids or animals, nothing like that 'cos I ain't no bleedin' pervert."

Fat Albert loved the job. Sat there in a nice warm office in a modern warehouse, down a quiet lane in deepest Essex with no bosses or customers to bother him anymore. A state-of-the-art Italian coffee-machine and a microwave oven sitting next to a well-stocked fridge satisfied his natural appetites while the internet satisfied his unnatural ones.

As for the 'work', that was easy. All he had to do was check the deliveries in, check them out again and pay the drivers. And make the odd phone call if things weren't quite right. Which they weren't today. In fact, Fat Albert thought, they were just about as wrong as they could possibly be. That, and his unintentional part in it all, upset him greatly.

But it wasn't the source of his confusion. That much is as clear as a bleedin' bell, he thought as he stared at the piece of new technology lying on the desk in front of him. He went to pick up the smart phone but as he did so, fag ash tumbled down the front of his cardigan. He jerked back and beat the front of his cardigan with both hands. Just imagine going home to Dor' with holes in me best cardy, he thought. The grief she'd given him last time.

"Watch that ash, Albert." She'd yelled. "Don't you dare get holes in that cardy. Cashmere it is. Cost a fortune!" Then buy me cheapo ones from down the market, he'd thought, but wisely, didn't say. Satisfied there were no holes, he picked up the 'phone. He stabbed at it with a huge forefinger as if that would bring it to life and show him what to do. He poked it again and, to his surprise, the screen lit up, asking him to enter the pass code.

Bollocks, he thought, what's that bleedin' code again? Then remembered that his ten-year-old granddaughter had written it down for him.

"Old people like you have to write things down, Grandad," she'd said, "Because your brains don't work that well anymore. I'd put it in a Word document on your PC, but you wouldn't have a clue how to get to it."

Being cheeky without meaning to and he'd laughed. Loving her for it. Got a bit about her already, that girl, he'd thought, proudly. Hope I'm still around when she grows up. Smiling at the memory now, he reached into the right-hand drawer of his desk and pulled out a notebook with "Grandad's Stuff. (Hands off everybody else!)" written on the front in her looping, child's hand. He tapped in the code, touched the screen twice more and heard her little voice in his head. 'Tap it, Grandad, don't poke at it like that. Tap!" He smiled as he waited while the number rang.

"Speak."

"Anthony? It's Albert."

"Yes, Albert, I know. Your name and number come up on screen on this phone, don't they?"

"Oh, yeah, right," Albert said, feeling like an idiot before he'd even started.

There was a short silence.

"So what is it Albert? I assume you didn't call me to ask me if I fancied Spurs against Arsenal tomorrow."

"No, no. It's still important though. It's today's delivery. Hate to tell you but there's a bit of a problem... well, big problem, really."

"Albert. Albert. Not on this phone, okay? How many bleedin' times I have to tell you? We use the burners for problems, remember? Ease your big arse outta that chair, grab the phone out of the cabinet and I'll call you back in two minutes."

Fat Albert did as he was told, eased his arse out of the chair and walked over to the filing cabinet by the window, stepping carefully over the man lying on the floor as he went. He pulled open the top drawer and took out a plain black mobile phone. So small, it almost disappeared in his meaty fist. Basic job. Calls and texts and pay as you go. Safe. Or so he was told. As if he'd know the difference. Or even care. The phone rang just as he got back to his desk. He poked the green phone thingy but didn't say anything.

"Okay, Albert," Anthony said with a sigh, "tell me exactly what the problem is and then we'll sort it."

"Won't be easy to sort this one, son. It's today's delivery, yeah? It's well... the goods... they're damaged."

"Damaged? What the hell you on about damaged?" Anthony said, his voice rising. "How many and how bad?"

"Damaged badly's what I mean, Tony. And all of 'em, actually. Sorry, son, but they can't be put right. None of this can."

"What? None of them? And what the hell do you mean by none of this?"

"What I said. None of it. They're too far gone, son. It's all gone tits up. All we can do is... what they call it these days... damage limitation? We need the cleaners."

"The cleaners? Jesus Christ, Albert, what the fuck's been goin' on?" Anthony said, shouting now.

"No don't say it, not even on this phone. I'll be over. Take me an hour. Shit, no, I've had a drink. I'll get George to drive me. Don't do anything, wait 'til I get there."

Fat Albert replaced the receiver and walked back into the office. He sat down in his chair, lit another cigarette and clicked into his favourite web site. And settled back to enjoy another session of Milfs and their anal sex habits.

Two

Almost an hour later he clicked out of the internet when he heard a car pull up. There were footsteps in the warehouse and then young Anthony's voice before he could see him.

"Albert! What the bleedin' hell's goin' on? The truck's still here and both the trailers. I know the goods are damaged so that trailer's stayin' but the truck should be well gone with the other one by now." He stopped talking when he reached the office and saw the man lying on the floor. "The bleedin' hell's this, Albert? Tired after his journey our Peter, was he? What's he, asleep?"

"Sleepin'? Nah. 'Fraid not, Tony. Dead ain't he," Albert said.

"Dead? What the…? How? Who?"

"Me. I killed him I mean," Albert said.

"You what…?"

"Hang on, hang on, didn't mean to, did I? Just tapped him with the bat at first, quiet him down a bit after he tried to 'ave me. Came back and finished him off after though when I saw what he'd done. The little shit."

"Finished him off? What? You say that like you know what it means, Albert. When've you ever finished anybody off, eh? Never, that's when. What you on about?"

"Couldn't help meself, could I. Not after I saw the damage he'd done."

"Fuck me, Albert," Anthony said, "all the goods're damaged, truck's still here, now you. You never done anybody in your life, never involved in any serious physicals, and you've only gone and topped the first one you have been involved with. And we've lost a driver as a result. You believe this, George?"

George just shook his head and nudged the body with his right foot.

"Got any good news for me 'ave you, Albert?" Anthony said.

Albert shook his head.

"Thought not. Okay, from the top, Albert." But then he held up his hand and nodded at the body.

"First things first, though. Take him out of 'ere, George, there's a good lad. Can't be lookin' at that while I'm listenin' to Albert's little tale. Then go sit in the motor and watch the yard."

George took hold of the driver's wrists and dragged him into the warehouse. Anthony closed the door and sat down facing Albert.

"Right, you. Tell me," he said. "Everything."

Three

Earlier that day.

Albert sat at his desk, trying to contain his anger. He was a simple man who liked things in order. Liked things to happen as they should and when they should. He liked to know. Today, though, none of those things were happening. Because the truck should have been here five hours ago and there'd been no phone call from the driver, Peter, to let him know what the score was. Peter the bleedin' Pole. The ferry was on time - first thing he'd done was check that - so where the hell was he?

He'd thought about phoning Anthony but decided against it. Didn't want to get a bollocking for bothering him before he knew what the problem was. So he stared into space, constantly checking his watch, even walking out into the yard a couple of times. The most pointless of all that was because he'd have to go back in to open the gates anyway.

He sat up when he heard the truck approaching. Prat, Albert thought as the sounds of the air brakes and air horn floated across the fields. How many times have I told him, use the gears, drive properly, leave off the horn. Don't let the whole bleedin' world know you're coming.

"Relax, Albert" he'd say. "You worry too much. We out in country here, nobody about, who cares?"

"I care, you dull Polish pillock," Albert had told him. "'Cos it ain't called 'bandit country' for nothin'. Being careful's what's kept me out of nick all me life and I ain't going inside for the first time just 'cos you don't open your bleedin' ears and listen."

But none of them listen these days, Albert thought. The old days are gone. Used to be family. All the sons, and sons of friends, steppin' up as the old boys dropped away. Didn't have to tell them anything much. Learned all the basics from the tit. Don't wanna know now though.

"Bleedin' HGV licence? Take me months to get that. Could earn fifty, sixty grand in that time."

And they could. Drugs. Cocaine mostly. All they was interested in. Brought in the money for the clothes, the cars and the girls. And the drugs themselves as well. Young arseholes. Couldn't just deal, could they? Had to have themselves a little taste. And you can't just have a taste, can you? They were useless inside a couple of years. Even if they hadn't been nicked, they were a hopeless mess. And if they did get nicked, you couldn't expect this generation to keep their mouths shut and just do their time.

So, you had all these east European guys instead. Guys brought in for the grunt work but who showed a bit of promise. And the Poles were the best of them. Knew the meaning of hard work. Could depend on them for that – and for a bit of plumbing and electrics - but no discipline in them. Too laid back for that. You had to tell them every bleedin' thing.

He heard the truck pull up in the lane and he pressed the button to open the gates. Heard the air brakes again as he parked. Peter the Pole put his head round the office door less than a minute later.

Eh? Too bleedin' quick, Albert thought as he slid Peter's wages back into the drawer. Nose twitching. And I didn't hear the trailers being switched, he thought. Something's off here.

"What's goin' on?" Albert said. "Why ain't you unloaded?

"No time Albert. Late. Got to go now," Peter said, not looking at him.

Jumpy, Albert thought. More than. And this one's normally cool as the proverbial.

"Hang on, hang on," he said. "Get your arse in 'ere, you. Siddown. What's up?"

Peter moved in from the doorway but didn't sit down. He's not just jumpy Albert thought, he's bleedin' twitching.

"I'll only ask you once more," Albert said, pointing a fat finger at him. "What's goin' on? And where you bin, son, eh? Five hours late you are. Five! Come on, what happened?"

"Trouble with ferry, Albert. Was late. And later with unloading," Peter said, looking more uncomfortable than ever.

Now Albert knew there was trouble. He sat up straight in his chair and reached for the cut-down baseball bat that was propped against the drawers.

"Don't take me for a cunt, son," Albert said. "I'm old, not stupid. First thing I did was check the ferry. Docked at 6:30 this mornin' on the dot. So I checked with our friendly DC, got him to look at the traffic pictures and guess what? There's your truck rollin' down the A12 alright, but last night, not this mornin'. Then it takes the turn off to Hatfield bleedin' Peverel. What? Her old man back out in Afghan, is he?'

Peter almost jumped back. "What you know about woman?"

"Ain't got a clue, 'ave you son?' Albert said, shaking his head. "We know everything about you and your dirty little habits. Dippin' your wick where you shouldn't. And you wanna be careful, son. You know what her old man is, don't you?

"Yes," Peter said. "Soldier."

Albert laughed and shook his head. "Yeah, but not just any old soldier my son. He's a sergeant with the Paras. And that means what him and his mates would do to you if he ever finds out you're knobbing his wife don't bear thinking about. You'd be beggin' them to kill you by the end. You didn't know, did you?" Albert said when he saw the expression on Peter's face.

"How you know so much?" Peter asked, voice shaking.

"What? You think we'd let you drive our goods, take care of valuable cargo without checking everything out first? Come on."

Peter turned and reached for the door handle as he spoke.

"Okay. So I have a little fun," he said. "She likes, I like. No big deal. Only go when he's out of country. No worry for you." He pulled the door open. "Got to go now, Albert, take other truck."

Albert stood up and walked round the desk, the bat hidden behind his legs.

"Hang on a mo' sunshine, you ain't goin' nowhere 'til we've sorted this. Show me the truck, lemme see what the score is here."

Albert took a step forward and Peter reached out, grabbed his lapels and tried to push him back. But at half the weight and six inches shorter he had no chance. He backed away and turned his shoulder, but Albert saw the intended punch coming a mile off.

For such a big man, his response was surprisingly quick. He lifted his arm, flicked his wrist and the bat smacked into the side of Peter's head just above his left ear. He didn't fall over, just folded, collapsed inwards like a puppet with its strings cut. He fell to his knees then slowly spread out on the floor.

Albert reached down and felt Peter's neck. A very faint pulse. Fuck me, he thought, didn't hit him all that hard. Poles got thin skulls or what? He went through the Peter's pockets, took his keys and the knife he kept in a special pocket inside his jacket. He put the knife on the desk and then walked slowly into the warehouse. A little concerned, worried even, but still relaxed. He kept hold of the bat, though. He stopped and picked up a pair of pliers to cut the seals on the truck doors. He walked outside and saw the truck.

It wasn't reversed in the bay ready to hook up to the next trailer, more like abandoned in the yard, the truck turned at an angle from its own trailer. Like a big mechanical tick, Albert thought, as he slammed the driver's door shut. He walked to the back of the trailer and took out the pliers. Then stopped and stared. The Customs seals were already broken, and the handles were in the open position.

He swapped the bat to his left hand, reached up and slowly pulled the door open. And recoiled when the smell hit him. The smell of blood and bodily fluids that covered the shapes that lay on the floor. Human shapes. Female human shapes.

His brain tilted, his stomach surged, and he dropped to his knees before vomiting the contents of his stomach – the contents of his soul, Albert thought – onto the concrete beneath him. He retched again and again until there was only bile left. He stayed down on all fours, tears and snot streaming down his face, until he was able to breathe more easily.

After a few long minutes he hauled himself to his feet, wiped his eyes and nose on his sleeve before clamping his handkerchief to his face. Then he looked in the trailer again. The shapes he'd seen were all those of young girls. Very young girls. Twelve or thirteen they looked, most of them. Released from the secret panels that ran the length of the trailer. Lying in small heaps on top of one another. Vomit on their faces and blood on their fingers. He suddenly realised they must have suffocated to death in there. Overnight and half the day without the air switched on. While Peter the fucking Pole was parked up, fucking his woman.

He pushed the doors to and without thinking about it, he walked back into the office, took the bat in both hands and hit Peter repeatedly over the head until he wasn't breathing any more. He threw the bat down, walked over to the cabinet behind his desk and took out the whisky bottle and a glass.

He filled the glass and took it with him into the kitchen. He took a large mouthful, gargled with it for a couple of minutes then spat it out into the sink. And did it again until the glass was empty, and his mouth and throat tasted of nothing other than whisky.

He walked back to his desk, filled the glass again, took another mouthful, this time savouring the taste before feeling the soothing burn as he swallowed the lot. Don't get this at all, he thought. He'd never seen what was in the trucks but always assumed it was some sort of goods, electronics maybe, to cover what was probably drugs. Cheap in the east and sold for huge profits in London. Never imagined anything like girls, kids really, and didn't understand what they were all about. Couldn't get his head round it.

Four

"And that's when I 'phoned you," Albert said, "because I didn't know what else to do."

"You did absolutely right Albert," Tony said, nodding towards Peter's body on the floor. "Fact is, if you hadn't, I would've done him meself."

"Weren't thinking really, I was so upset," Albert said. "And once I'd started I couldn't stop, could I? Weren't able to help meself. Sorry Anthony."

"Nothing to be sorry about, Albert. And don't worry, we'll get this sorted, 'phone the cleaners, then get out of here."

Albert nodded. "Knew you'd sort it, son."

"One more thing though. Did you climb inside the truck?"

"What? No, couldn't stand the sight and smell, could I? Saw the girls, smelled them, and that was enough. Just got out of there and spewed me guts up."

"Check if any were still alive, did you?"

"Christ no, Anthony. Couldn't 'ave paid me to go back in that truck again, never mind touch any of 'em."

"Right, but we still gotta check it out."

"Your jokin', son," Albert said. "I ain't goin' in that truck. No chance."

"Okay, maybe not inside," Anthony said but you're comin' with me. Come on."

Albert followed Anthony out to the truck but he stayed outside, a hanky over his nose and mouth while Anthony climbed up and squeezed into one of the compartments. He appeared less than a minute later, bent over and threw up on the floor of the truck. Albert waited until he'd gathered himself.

"Bad in there, is it?" he asked.

"Bad?" Anthony said, wiping tears from his eyes. "Worse than bad, Albert. They're all dead Albert. Every last one of em' Never smelled anything like it. There ain't gonna be no profit from this run."

"Profit? What you on about profit?"

Anthony shook his head. "Is it too simple a word for you, Albert, profit? You know, buy for less, sell for more. Difference is profit, yeah? Ain't too difficult to understand, is it?

"So what're you sayin', they get sold on?"

"Yes, of course they do Albert. We don't bring 'em over 'ere out of the goodness of our hearts now, do we? We sell 'em on to people who need them for their business."

"Prossies, you mean?"

"Well yeah, sort of," Anthony said. "Not the way you're probably thinking though. But working girls, yeah."

"Then we gotta do something about it, Anthony. We gotta put a stop to this," Albert said, shouting again.

"Whoa, whoa. Hang on a minute, Albert. Do something? About what, exactly? What are you on about?"

"This trafficking. Bringing young girls in, sellin' them to who knows who. It's not on. We gotta stop them, Anthony."

Anthony shook his head again, wondering about Albert's lack of nous. "Stop them? There ain't no them, Albert. Them is us! We're them, one's that's doin' it."

"Truckin' them in, yeah, using our trucks and drivers sure. But who's paying us to do it? Whose business is it?"

"Whose business? Jesus Albert. This shock's done your brain in. It's our business you bleedin' idiot. And it's a profitable one an' all. The most profitable we've ever bin involved in. I'll tell you that."

"But using girls that young? Fucking children's what they are. And that ain't right. We gotta do something about it."

"They're not young girls, not children." Tony said, doing his best to stay calm and patient. Not what I got out of bed for this morning, he thought.

"You gotta stop thinkin' of them like that, Albert. Young girls. 'Cos they ain't. They're just merchandise, is all. Okay, they're live, not boxes of stuff, but still just merchandise."

"Merchandise! You what?" Albert shouted. "That all you got say about it? Fucking merchandise? Can't believe what I'm fucking hearing."

"Calm down Albert, calm down will you. And no, it ain't all I got to say. Not by a long shot. 'Cos they're profit as well. Lots of it. It's a huge earner for the family. Including you, don't forget."

"Profit? An earner? Dirty bleedin' earnings you mean. And it ain't right, this. It's a filthy fucking business and we shouldn't be in it. Not when it kills people - young girls."

"Hate to tell you Albert, me old son, but you've been involved in worse."

"What me?" Albert said, shocked. "No I ain't. Never."

"Albert, what you think went in and out the back of that pub all those years you were running it?"

"Hookey gear of course."

"Yeah, thirty, forty, years ago when my old man was just startin' out. But not now. It's been guns and drugs for a long time now... that's right Albert, guns and drugs is what it mainly was and if you don't think they kill people, and a lot more than died last night, then you're softer in the head than I thought. Like I said, this is more profitable than anything we've ever done before, so you just forget about doin' anything, okay?"

"But what about the guys who pick them up in the first place?"

"Pick them up? You think our guys, and yes, wipe that stupid look off your face, they're our guys, we employ them, we use them, you think they just pull 'em off the streets? Think that wouldn't get us noticed? Guys in a van pulling young 'uns off the streets in foreign parts..."

"So how do we get 'em then?"

"How d'you think? We buy them Albert. Pay good money for them."

"Eh? Albert said, shocked again. "But who's got young girls like this to sell? he asked. "I don't get it."

Anthony forced himself to stay calm. Took a couple of deep breaths and said, "Who owns young girls, Albert, girls of ten to fifteen? Go on, who?"

Albert thought for a minute or two. "Their parents? Family?"

"Got it in one," Anthony said. "Their bleedin' parents. Can't wait to get the money in their dirty little paws, a grand a time, and unload the girls on us. And how many of them girls are virgins when we get them, Albert, eh? Even the ten-year-olds. How many d'you think?"

"Nah. Ten-year-olds? You're just windin' me up now."

"Wish I was," Anthony said. "But I ain't. We pay premium for the virgins, pay way more than we do for the others, one's that've been serviced already."

"At ten?" Albert shouted. "Who shags ten-year-old girls for gawd's sake?"

Anthony grimaced and raised his eyebrows in silent question.

Albert suddenly understood. "Hang on a mo'… their *families*? That what you're sayin'?"

"Give the man a big fat cigar. Yes, their families Albert, who'd you think," Anthony said. "Their fathers, brothers, uncles, cousins. Who else would it be? They get broken in and shared around. Believe me, most of 'em know what it's all about by the time they get here. Even at ten, most of 'em, they've had everything done to them you can think of and a bit more."

"I can't get me head round this," Albert said. "Don't know where to start with it. Bring these girls over here, after all that's happened to them, just to put them on the street?"

"On the street? You mad, Albert? There's plenty others do that sort of shit. Scrape a living from girls they do compared to us. Our girls never see the street. What? You think they're stuck in leather minis up to their arses, crop tops and five-inch heels and paraded up and down the pavements behind Kings Cross. Jesus! This is not some low-rent operation we're talking here."

Anthony shook his head, poured himself a whisky. Took a large swallow.

"Okay, okay," he said, controlling his voice even thought all he wanted to do was hit the old man. Preferably with the baseball bat.

"Let me explain the facts of life to you, Albert, because you need to understand this. You really do. What do you think these girls are worth to us, in pure hard cash?"

"No idea, have I?" Albert mumbled.

"No, 'course you 'aven't. Well let me explain it to you Albert. Thirty-five grand a time, that's what. Twenty a trip at thirty-five grand each is seven hundred thou'. One trip a month, every month, is eight and a half mil a year. Eight and a half… million… quid. Say it slowly. Got it now? And you want to do something about it?"

"No, you shut your face," Anthony said when Albert started to protest. "Just shut it and let me tell you the facts of life here. We pay good money for these girls, 'specially the virgins like I said. Because we get better money for them in return. This ain't the street, this is private clubs, we're talking. Exclusive."

"Fuck me," Albert said. "And I was thinking twenty quid blow jobs."

"Jesus Christ almighty," Anthony said, shaking his head. "Look we pay a lot for these girls, and because of that, we don't ask them to freeze their arses off out in the street. No real profit in that. And anyway, what's Old Bill gonna do if they see ten-year olds on the street in full view? The usual toms, well, they pretty much turn a blind eye to them unless they're causing a real nuisance, which most of 'em have learned not to do, but they wouldn't if they saw children out there now would they."

"So what happens, instead then?" Albert asked, totally confused.

"They work in exclusive clubs and private houses, that's what. And they live in houses with matrons. Madams if you like, except they're not involved in any business dealings, just there to look after the girls. And nice houses as well, no pokey, damp back-street flats. Nice beds, three to a room okay, but they're clean, and good food as well, nice clothes, everything. They're properly looked after. Better than living in poxy little villages in Romania, Serbia or Transylfuckingvania wherever it is they come from. Better here clean and fed than living in shit being serviced by their brothers, fathers whatever."

"You honestly believe that do you?" Albert asked.

"Yes, Albert, I do," Anthony said, controlling himself more than he thought possible. "Because it's true. Listen to me, and you're gonna listen, I'll tell you exactly why. Their life is way better here, Albert. And don't shake your head at me like that! Back home they got no hope, none at all. But here? They ain't starving and okay, so they got to service some old geezer couple of times a week, lay on their backs, kneel down, whatever, and think of the fucking Pope, yeah, but that's still better than being raped in the dirt by their own family and then have to crawl off to some filthy freezin' bed. And before you say anything, we take them that young because eighteen is too old at this end of the business. Ten to fourteen's what they really want and why they pay prime rates at the clubs. Because the guys who are in the know, who get to use these girls, they're not ordinary punters. Not your average kerb-crawlers. They're MPs, Judges, top level businessmen, top coppers, you know, the usual suspects."

"Now you really are winding me up," Albert said.

"Christ almighty, Albert, where you been living? Things haven't changed much since old Ma Payne and her luncheon vouchers back in the Seventies. Who else's got the sort of money to pay for these girls? Not punters on the streets that's for sure. It's rich people, Albert. They're the ones. Sort who don't have to worry where the next million's coming from. And those sorts of guys? They don't want twenty-odd year-old skanks wrecked by smack with track marks up and down their arms and legs. They want young flesh. Younger the better. Looked after properly. Clean and fresh smelling nice and looking good and healthy."

Anthony shook his head and sighed.

"Look, we ain't selling them on to scum. The guys who buy the girls from us, one's that own the houses and run the clubs? They're English guys. Upper class some of them. Maybe even a Royal or two I've been told. Run these private, very private clubs. No advertising, all word of mouth, know what I mean? You only know about them if you're in the know. And you're only in the know if you're already a member of their very exclusive club. It's called The Establishment. Heard of it? No proles allowed. The girls have to be young and look good because they cost ten grand a night, more for the youngest virgins, and they do a couple of nights a week. Do the numbers, okay Albert? We bring in twenty a trip. Means they've got twenty girls, ten grand a night each, two nights a week minimum? Four hundred grand right there. The money they paid us for them? They've got it back in the first coupla weeks. Are you starting to get the bleedin' message, uncle?

Albert just stared. "Bleedin' hell, Anthony, never heard you speechify like that before."

"Yeah, well, you needed to know."

"What I do know is they all died tonight, all twenty of 'em. Could've been my granddaughter in there. Ever think of that?"

"No, Albert, I don't. Because we look after our kids way better than these people. Because we can afford to. So it would never happen. Listen, this was the first time anything's gone wrong," Anthony said. "And it'll be the last. It was Peter's screw up, that's all. So don't you think about doing anything," he said, poking Albert hard in the chest. "And don't you say anything about this to anybody. Not even people inside the firm, never mind outside. But especially the coppers. 'Specially them. Because if you do, I won't be responsible. Never mind you're my uncle and my godfather, I'll fucking deal with you myself. Yeah? We understand each other here Albert?"

"Yeah, I hear you."

"You hear me, but are you *listening*, Albert? Really listening? And understanding what I'm tellin' you?"

"Yeah, yeah, I get it," Albert mumbled. "No, I do," he said when Anthony poked him in the chest again. "Leave off with that. I get it."

"Well, then," Anthony said, "let's get this sorted and get off out of here. Come on, lock up, I gotta make a couple of calls."

He took out a throw-away mobile and thumbed in a number.

"It's me," he said. "Got a job for you. Urgent." He paused. "The warehouse. Twenty-one items, two trucks and trailers." He paused again. "Cost me? Well I didn't think I was phoning the Salvation fucking Army, did I? Just you get here sharpish and get it done. Items gone, and I mean gone. Totally. Trucks and trailers are yours on top of the fee."

He ended the call, dropped the phone to the floor took out the battery and sim card and stomped the case to pieces. Gathered them up and put them in his pocket. He turned to Albert.

"Get in the Jag, you can drop me at my old man's, George'll pick me up from there."

"George!" he shouted. "Over here. Now." George strolled over from the Range Rover. "Got some jobs for you. Wait for the cleaners, there's money in the safe to pay them. Whatever they ask. Then bug that office phone…. and the office and kitchen as well. I want to know everything's said in there from now on. Then check with our friendly DC, make sure we know, soon as, if they get any iffy calls about all this bollocks. And tomorrow, first thing, sort out Peter's woman. Then you can…"

"Whoa, whoa, steady on boss, I can't keep up with you, you got to talk slower…."

"No, George, I don't. You got to listen quicker. The money, the cleaners, the bugs and our friendly DC. With me so far?"

"Yeah, but Peter's woman? What's…"

"Sort her, I said. Permanently. Christ alone knows what Peter's told her when their heads were together on the pillows afterwards. And make it look like a robbery gone wrong. Make sure she's out of bed when you do it. Hammer, knife, whatever, but no gun. Your average robbers don't use guns out here. Okay?"

George nodded. "Okay. I get that. No worries. But I thought there was something else you wanted."

"Thought? What's that? What've we agreed you're good at George, eh?"

George grinned. "Driving and doing what I'm told. Getting things sorted properly."

"That's right. So just do what I said, okay? Then come over to my old man's and pick me up. Albert's dropping me. Want to make sure he goes home, doesn't do anything silly today. Okay?"

"Twice in a day at your old man's? Sure that'll be okay with him?" George asked.

"Don't start with all that, George. I know my old man's a bit old-school, but he accepts you're sound 'cos I say so, and mum loves you, doesn't care you're Black. And if she says you're the dogs', what's my old man gonna say, eh? Fuck all, that's what. So get yourself over later and fetch me."

"Okay," Anthony said. "See you later."

Anthony walked over to the Jaguar and slid into the passenger seat.

"Right Albert," he said, "you okay to drive?" Albert nodded. "Okay then, take me to Dad's then you get straight off home. Get a good night's sleep and we'll talk again in the morning."

"Same as usual tomorrow then?"

"No, Albert. Ring me on my mobile before you leave the house. I'll let you know if everything's okay for you to go in. Should be, but just in case, eh?"

Albert nodded but said nothing. Just kept his hand on the ignition key.

"You good with all this, Albert? You keepin' in mind what I said?"

"Yeah, I'm good. Just take a couple of days to get me head round this. But you needn't worry. I'm good."

"Okay then. You gonna start this motor or what?"

"In a minute," Albert said. "There's a coupla things been niggling away at me. Something we ain't bin thinkin' about here."

"Oh, yeah, and what's that then, Einstein?"

"You ain't askin' the why."

"Why, what, Albert?" Anthony asked, irritation in his voice. "What you on about?"

Albert eased his bulk around to face his nephew. "First thing, Peter said he was gonna take the truck out. But he never does that. Janusz takes it and Peter rides with him. So why ain't Janusz turned up to take the truck out as usual? He knows the routine and he's always here ready. 'Bout half an hour before the truck arrives. Good kid. Like clockwork he is. But no sign of him today, is there? So we have to wonder why's that."

Anthony nodded, while he thought about what Albert had said. "You know you're right uncle. Hadn't thought about that with all this nonsense goin' on. Possible he could just have been delayed?"

"Nah," Albert said, shaking his head. "Good as gold, that one. Twice he's been held up and 'phoned me both times. And he's what? Seven or eight hours late. Nah, he ain't held up, gone awol, more like."

"Yeah, you're right. But why?" Anthony asked. "That's the question. Why today?"

"Yes, it is," Albert said. "You believe in coincidence?"

"No I bleedin' don't. Not in this business anyway."

"Nor me," Albert said. "So I reckon he's up to no good as well. And that surprises me more than Peter."

He paused and drummed his fingers on the steering wheel.

"But there's an even bigger question, Anthony and it's a killer."

"Yeah? And what's that?"

"Why Peter switched off the refrigeration system, which also killed the air supply, that's what."

"Eh? That's not a mystery. It's 'cos he parked up overnight. The truck was switched off for about twelve hours, maybe more."

"That wouldn't have done it though. Not how those big fridge trucks work, is it?"

"It isn't?"

"Nah. Look, it's common sense. They're on the ferry for bleedin' hours and trucks aren't allowed to keep their engines runnin', same as cars. So how'd they keep stuff cool unless the refrigeration keeps workin' when the engine's switched off? Must run off a different system. Don't ask me what, but it has to. Get me? So for all the girls to suffocate, he had to switch the system off, didn't he?"

There was a long silence while Anthony thought it all through. Then he turned to look at his uncle. "Y'know, Albert, sometimes you ain't as dumb as you look," he said. "A chap could underestimate you, he wasn't careful."

Albert looked embarrassed. "Yeah, well, I 'ave me moments."

"And you just had one. 'Cos you're absolutely right. So... he switched it off, knowing there'd be no air for the girls. So why? Why would he do that? He knew we'd find out, we'd 'ave him for it, so why? Why wouldn't he be scared of us? Don't make no sense."

He paused again, nodding while he tried to work it out. "What was Peter interested in, Albert?" he eventually said.

"Money," Albert said without hesitation. "All he ever talked about. Looking to get a big enough wedge together to buy 'imself a truck was what he always wanted. Even asked me if we would allow that and I told him no reason we wouldn't."

He paused for a minute or two. Anthony could almost hear the gears grinding in Albert's head, so he waited patiently.

"You know what," Albert said, "I reckon somebody must've paid him. That'd do it alright. Somebody we'd think twice about goin' up against an' all. We ain't the biggest firm around but we frighten enough people. How would he dare do one on us if the other mob aren't well tasty?"

"Yeah, but who? We're not stepping on the toes of any of the real big boys, dad made sure of that when he set all this up. So who'd want to screw up our little operation?"

"Didn't know we had any competition," Albert said.

"That's the problem, we ain't. Or none that I know of - and I'd know, believe me."

"Your dad know? Like you said, he set you up with all this, didn't he? So he'd know the guys that're behind it all, yeah?"

"Yeah, you're right again Albert. I've met the managers, guys that run things, but I've never met the guys, the public-school twats, that own it all. Right, drop me of at my old man's Albert and I'll have a chat with him."

Five

Anthony and his dad sat in the front room of the old family house. His dad in his favourite armchair, Anthony sitting facing him on the other side of the fireplace. Neither man spoke when Anthony's mum came in carrying a tray which held two cups of tea and a plate of home-made cake. Drinking bleedin' tea, Anthony thought. Only because mum won't allow hard liquor, or beer even, in the house since the old man's heart trouble.

"Yeah, I miss it, of course I do", his dad had said when Anthony asked him about the lack of booze.

"But she's the guv'nor in here. Way it is, way it's always been. I run the business, she runs the house and family. Call me sexist these days I s'pose. Sensible use of talent's what I say. She'd no interest in the business and she managed the house and you four a sight better than I ever could. Fact the other three are well out of it's down to her. You still bein' in the business is down to her an' all - and what you were of course."

"*He's lost already*" she told me when you was about 10. "*Not even gonna bother trying to set him straight anymore. No point. He'll join you in the business but you better look out for him, John Joseph Foley, or else*".

"And you know your mum's serious when she says, "or else". You take it serious or take your lumps."

"And when she calls you John Joseph Foley," Anthony said with a wink, "you *know* she's serious and you better do it. And she still only ever calls you John," he added.

"Yea, rest of the world calls me Jack, but for her, it's John. Hates Jack - and anybody calls you Tony. And like you said, it's "John Joseph" when I'm in trouble," he said with a grin. "Just like my Mum used to."

"Yeah, I know. But dad… about today."

"Oh, yeah. Sorry I'm rambling. Two problems you said? Let's be 'avin' them then. See if we can't sort somethin' out."

Anthony explained what had happened to the truck, the girls and Peter. And Janusz's no show.

"What? Albert did 'im?" his father said. "Albert? Bloody hell, Anthony. Big as he is, he's never done anybody in his life. Never. That'll have properly upset him, that will."

"Don't think it's really sunk in yet, dad. He was in a bit of a daze earlier, but his brain was working fine, things he'd worked out. Right on the money, I reckon."

He explained Albert's theory about the truck and the refrigeration system and his questions about Peter and Janusz. His father didn't say anything for five minutes. Anthony settled back in his chair and waited.

"Okay," his father said finally. "You were there, what d'you reckon. Albert got it right, you think?"

"About the truck? Pretty sure, yeah," Anthony said. "System must've been switched off. Peter's the only one who could've done it and Albert tells me the way he was acting was well sus. So yeah, gotta think he was at it alright. And Janusz as well. Not showing up at all and no call? I mean, first time ever, got to put him right in it."

"Yeah, I reckon," his father said. "And paid to do it Albert thinks?"

"Yeah. And I agree with him. Can't see why else he would do it. Problem is, I can't think who'd do that. Who'd be after our business? 'Cos what we've paid out already for the girls, the bill for the cleaners plus the trucks and what we're gonna have to pay in compensation? Hard to swallow that. Plus, we'd have to find replacements for Peter and Janusz. I just can't figure it, dad. I thought you had everything sorted. Thought we'd be safe from naughties like this."

"I had, yeah," his father said, "but things have changed lately."

Anthony sat up. "Changed? How?"

"Change in ownership. The guys we've been dealing with the past coupla years, them that used to own everything? Well, they had to sell out a good few months ago. Didn't want to mind, but they weren't given no option, the sort of guys who were buyin'... it weren't exactly an offer if you know what I mean."

"Shit," Anthony said. "A few months?" His father nodded. "Means they've had enough time to get a proper handle on the business if they're sharp enough. Who are these guys? D'you know?"

"Oh yeah. I've met 'em. Met the main man a couple of times. Russians they are. And yes, they're well sharp."

"Russians?" Anthony said. "You never said. Since when have the Russians got the class and the connections to run this business?"

His dad shook his head. "Nah, ain't the old squint-eyed, knuckle-draggers you're thinking about, Anthony. Not the thugs we've had to deal with in the past. They ain't like the Albanians. These're the new lot. Smooth as. Handmade everything. Suits, shirts, shoes, even their bleedin' teeth. Rollers and Bentleys, not second-hand Audis and BMWs. They got everythin' to make 'em look respectable. Smooth talkin', but plenty muscle to back up the words, I can tell you."

"So, was it them you think?" Anthony asked.

"Seems like. Nobody else knows our business, not in any detail anyway. Gonna have to make a call, Anthony. Gimme half an hour or so. You go chat to your mum in the kitchen. Close both doors and keep her in there."

Anthony walked through to the kitchen where his mum was busy baking and chatting to George. He put his hands on her hips and kissed the top of her head.

"You off, then son?" she said turning to face him. Anthony backed away to stop her putting her flour-covered hands on his suit.

"Nah. Dad's got a call to make. Private. So I've come in here to bother you. And no, I ain't doing no mixing for you. But I'll be a good boy and make us all a cuppa if you let me lick the bowl."

George laughed as she flicked the back of Anthony's head with the tea towel.

John Joseph Foley took a small notebook from his cardigan pocket and flipped through the pages. Then he picked up his mobile and tapped in a number. His call was answered but nobody spoke.

"John Foley," he said. "To speak to Yuri."

"Yuri not here," a heavily accented voice told him.

"Don't piss me about, son. You tell him who it is and he'll tell you himself whether he's there or not."

There was a further silence then a series of clicks before a man spoke.

"John, Joseph, my friend! And how are you today? You were on my list to call but you got me first! What can I do for you?'

After the first time they'd met, John Foley had wondered why Yuri called him by both his names. So he'd asked him.

"In Russia, is a sign of friendship." Yuri had said. `You know a man well, you like him, you often call him by his first name and then the patronymic. Mine is Yuri Ivanovich – but you can call me Yuri. Because I like you, John Joseph. You are good man."

So John had asked Yuri why he liked him.

"In this country of yours, I am used to dealing with small men, with small views. Only see what's in front of them and become stupid when you tell them you're taking it away. But you're a big man, you see big picture. You know you cannot fight me but you stand up, tell me what you want. You won't take less. You don't back down. Yet you are reasonable. And show respect. I like that in a man. I like you, John, Joseph. We shall do business together. We shall be friends. And friendship is the most important thing in Russia. You are my tovarich, yes?"

John remembered all this and decided to ask the question outright.

"I'll get straight to it, Yuri. You can tell me if you or your people had anything to do with the disaster that happened today with our latest delivery? Looked like an attempt to put us out of business." He paused for a moment, expecting an instant reply, but there was just silence, so he continued.

"I thought of you but wasn't sure because you know if you'd wanted my business, all you had to do was ask and we would've agreed a fair price."

There was another silence. Then a further series of clicks. Cutting people out of the conversation or including a few more, Foley wondered. Thinking it but not saying.

"Ah, yes, John Joseph, I thought this was it. It is reason I wanted to call you also. Some weeks ago I said your business should belong to me, said I wanted it, and one of my people took me to mean he should take it for me. Not my intention to do it this way and he has been dealt with."

"Dealt with?"

"No longer work for me. Not work for anybody anymore." He laughed. "Like your Pole, Peter, yes?"

John Foley almost dropped the 'phone. How the bleedin' hell did he know about that, he wondered.

Reading his mind, Yuri said, "Janusz, he work for me some time now, okay? And yes, I want your business, I can develop many ways. More women I can get from Russia, Estonia, Latvia, Lithuania than you can think. And I have ten truck companies, you only one. But I want buy from you. I am not like those bloody Russians you deal with before. Not thug like them. Always fight and kill to get what they want. Create disturbance, yes? I want life to be normal, no fighting, no police, no reporters. To take over things, how do you say it, "under the radar". Because quiet business is profitable business, yes? So let us talk about price, my friend. What do you think is reasonable?"

"First off," John said, "I think I'm due being paid on that load today. If your man hadn't stuck his oar in, we'd have delivered everything safe and sound and collected on it."

"That's reasonable, John Joseph. I agree."

"As for the rest of our business, I'd want a fair price and a couple of months to sort everything. We're off to Spain, for good, all the family, and I want to leave everything kosher. No loose ends to keep people worrying. And I'm just suggesting here, Yuri, not demanding, you understand. I know you could just take it all and pay me nothing if you wanted," he said, mentally crossing his fingers. Nowhere near as confident as he sounded.

"Yes, but I would not do that. Like I said, I am not thug. Want no problem with the police. What is it you say, "*make no waves*"? Everything neat, finished, tied off, would be best for me as well, I think. Let me see... would... six million pounds, for everything be satisfactory to you?"

John Foley smiled to himself. Oh, very satisfactory he thought. But on the basis that you never accept anybody's first offer, let's push it a bit, see what happens.

"Six mil? Tell you what, Yuri, with the profit on today's run added on, how we take it up to ten million? That would seem fairer to me.'

Yuri laughed. "Let us say we go in between and agree eight million, yes?"

"You're on, Yuri. But a single payment, no instalments. Okay?"

"Ah, John Joseph, you are a man close to my heart. Thirty years younger I would be making you work for me. Yes?"

"Working with you, you mean. Together."

Yuri laughed even louder. "Of course, of course. With, of course, with. But keeping a very close eye, yes? Otherwise, I wake up one morning and suddenly I have nothing. Or maybe not wake up at all, eh?" He laughed again. "But yes, eight million would be fine with me. I make that back in couple of months only. So. We have a deal, yes?"

"Yes, we have a deal, Yuri. I'll let you know the details of the next run and then we need to meet and sort out the rest of the business. And only you and me, okay, Yuri. No go-betweens. Stop any misunderstandings."

"Okay. Yes. Is good. And I give my word, this will not be interfered with. I tell all my people, anybody interfere with you, they interfere with me. Yes? And I will let you know where we shall meet. Okay?"

"Okay, Yuri. Good talking to you. Speak soon."

"Dasvidaniya my friend."

John Foley put the phone back in his pocket and realised his hand was sweating. But a result, he thought. Better than anything I'd thought possible. And felt relief. Spain. Settled. It was all within reach now.

Anthony was still chatting to his mum and George half an hour later when his dad called him back through. And gave him the thumbs up when he walked in the room with George a couple of paces behind.

"George," his dad said. "This stuff with Albert. You were there. Our Anthony got it right, you reckon."

"Yeah, I reckon so, Mr F. Seemed well unsettled, he did. And I've never heard him say things like he did today."

The old man nodded and sighed.

"Anyway, you get it sorted?" Anthony asked.

"Yeah, all sorted. Spoke to Yuri, the main guy."

"What's he like, then?"

"Like every other rich geezer you ever saw. He's got the clothes, the hair, the Bentley, the mansion in Kensington, the lot. Wouldn't know he was Russian at all 'cept for the accent - and the steel underneath it all of course. His two closest guys are ex-KGB, guys that would cut you into little bits like they'd cut their steak in a restaurant. With about as much feeling. I wouldn't cross him for anything. I'm kinda glad all this has happened in a way 'cos I don't feel easy with these guys. Things they do without blinking I'd never even think of doing. Couldn't stomach it. They make the old gangs look like boy scouts."

"So was it him and his lot today?"

"Yes and no. Told me it was one of his guys did it wantin' to please the boss. Said he knew nothing about it until it was all over."

"And you believe him?"

"Yeah, I do as it happens, son. He trusts me and I trust him. And he likes me he said. You believe that? He could squash us like flies but lets us off 'cos he likes me? Never understand those guys. Never."

"So what now?"

"He's agreed to pay us what we would've got for this run. And compensate us for upheaval and loss of business. Asked me if I thought six mil' was reasonable."

"You snapped his hand off I hope."

"Not bleedin' likely. You never want to seem too eager, Anthony. Never let them think they can take you cheap. I accepted his proposal but asked for ten, settled for eight."

Anthony was impressed. "That's a right result and no mistake dad. So what next?"

"We sell off what we've got, the other businesses, the properties, then the pub. Get another ten mil' easy for it all, way property prices have gone. Never thought I'd ever like bleedin' gentrification but it's puttin' cash in our pockets. Then we sort everything else out and off to Spain. I told him it would take a couple of months to get it done if we were left alone. Got a meetin' with him next week, see what he wants to buy."

"You sayin' it's early retirement for me as well?" Anthony said. "Didn't think it'd happen this early." He thought for a moment. "You know, I dunno what I think about that to be honest, dad."

"Well there might just be a place for you with Yuri, son, 'cos he's impressed with the way the business runs. And you got all the contacts. Want me to have a word with him next week?"

"If you think it'd be right for me, yeah, I'd listen to what he has to offer. Better than retiring to Spain with the old folk. And George. I'd want him as my driver and such. George?"

George nodded. "Like you said, Anthony, better than the old folk's home in Spain."

"Cheeky little sods, the pair of you," his dad said, grinning. "But what about today. About Albert?"

"I dunno how to put this, dad, but that stuff today seemed to throw him right off. And the things he was saying? I weren't happy with that at all."

His dad sighed and shrugged his shoulders.

"Our Albert. What can I tell you son? Your mum was always keen for him to retire proper when he finished with the pub. Wanted her brother safe and settled out in Spain. Should've listened to her, I should."

He sighed, stood up and walked across to the window. He stared down at the traffic for a while before turning back to face Anthony.

"That was his mark, son. Running the pub. The orderin', keepin' the staff in line, chattin' to the customers. Weren't interested in the stuff went in and out the back rooms and cellar. Never touched it, never even saw it probably. Thought of himself as a publican he did. Believe that?" he said, shaking his head.

"Knew I owned it, me, a villain, 'course he did. Knew villains used it all the time, knew the back rooms and cellar were full of hookey gear – and worse, though he never knew that bit. But he never thought that made him a villain. Didn't think like the rest of us."

He laughed. "I run a boozer," he used to say. "Name on the licence. Above the door. You're at it, Jack, yeah, keeps you busy an' all. What keeps me busy is runnin' this boozer. Don't have to worry about havin' my collar felt."

"What? Like they'd leave him out if they'd lifted you?" Anthony said. "That'd be right."

"Yeah, yeah, but he was never the brightest, was he, our Albert. Knew when I married your mum I'd never be able to use him proper. Not even as a heavy. Got the size for it but not the heart. He's a nice man your uncle Albert. Genuine. Know when he had his last fight?"

Anthony shook his head and waited for the reminiscing. He loved it when his dad got going on the old stuff.

"When he was nine," his dad said. "First time he learned how to use his size was his last fight. He was always a big kid, huge, six feet and 15 stone by fourteen he was, but he learned, at nine, just grab 'em and crush 'em. They couldn't nut him, even at nine he was too tall, and they couldn't break his grip. No point in them bringin' in their big brothers 'cos he was bigger than any of them. Twice the size, however old they were. All I had to do was tap him on the shoulder before he killed the little bastards. After that they left him alone 'til somebody new tried it and he had to crush them an' all."

"You know I forgot you've known him since you was kids," Anthony said. "Always seemed to come with mum somehow."

"Yeah, same hospital we was born in, grew up in the same slum flats and went to the same schools. Anyway, later, when he was six five and twenty-four stone, who's gonna have a go? 'Cept with a shooter of course, 'cos then, what good's it being able to crush 'em? So, I couldn't give him no heavy work. But he was pure gold to me. Kept the pub dead straight. Made sure there were no drugs used or sold on the premises. And he was big enough to keep any of the usual customers in line. Kept it clean. What is it, "kept an orderly house" is how they say it? Honest man, honest name on the licence, honest face for the coppers. And the coppers loved him. Quietest pub in the manor, never any problems to sort out. And all they could drink for free. He had it sorted."

"You should've sent him to Spain, though," Anthony said, "when he couldn't cope any more. His knees and back and everything."

"Yeah, yeah. I know, I know. Should've sent him over there like your Mum wanted. But would he go? Not on your bleedin' life. *"Leave the manor? Me mates? Only see Spurs on poxy Sky knowin' some poncey posh git's got me season ticket? Fuck that for a game of soldiers."*

Anthony laughed. "That sounds like him alright."

"Your Mum even had a go at him. Still wouldn't. Dor' even begged him, said she'd divorce him, if he didn't go, but he never took any notice of her before and he just called her bluff on that one. So I gave him the warehouse to look after. Safe. He'd see the trucks comin' in and out but never see the goods. Same as the pub. Knew it weren't kosher but hadn't a clue what it was. 'Til now. This bleedin' nonsense today. Peter the fuckin' Pole. If Albert hadn't topped him, I'd have done it meself. And he's all upset you say?"

"More than. Never heard him like this. Ever," Anthony said. "Keeps saying we gotta do something about it, gotta put a stop to the trafficking. Young girls. Sickens him he says. And he keeps on about his granddaughter. Don't know what he'll do, who he's liable to talk to. I'm worried, I tell you."

His dad shook his head. "No, no, no," he said. "That's bollocks. Albert knows the score even if he doesn't know what the full game is. He'd never grass me up, ever, so stop talkin' silly."

"I dunno dad, serious, you should've heard him." Anthony said. "You know I'd never say this about him if I wasn't properly worried. Look, he's never been a thinking man, has he? Always did what he was told. Reacted to things without thinking. Didn't look at himself, what he was doin' or think how it was affecting him. Life was simple to him. Just followed instructions without questioning them. But he's asking questions now and it scares me. He's talking about doing something. You know what could happen, a word in the wrong ear and we could be done for. You know what that DCI Clarke's like. He's got a real hard on for us…"

"Oi!" his Mum shouted from the kitchen, "I heard that! Less of that in my house, young man."

"Sorry, Ma," Anthony said. "Forgot where I was for a minute."

"Yeah, well… just sayin'."

His dad grinned at him and winked.

"It ain't funny dad, he's talking weird stuff I tell you. If he talks…"

"He won't," his father said. "Trust me on that. And anyway, what if he did? He's family. My brother-in-law for gawd's sake. I couldn't touch him. Not me. No, Albert'll die of natural causes before he'd grass. Heart. That'll do for him, shouldn't wonder. Don't worry, son. I'll 'ave a word and sort it. Tell him we're sellin' the business. That'll calm him down. I'll tell him tomorrow. And I'll make sure he's safely out of the way in a few days."

He turned away from Anthony and finished his tea. Anthony nodded to George, and they left the room. He walked into the kitchen and kissed his Mum.

"Something I should know about, Anthony?" she asked.

"Nah, Mum, bit of business is all."

"Could always tell when he was lying," she said, smiling at George. "His dad couldn't, but I could. Go on now, I'll get it from your dad later anyway. You look after him for me George, there's a good lad."

"Always Mrs F. Always," George said as the two men turned, left the house and climbed into the car.

"That's that, then," George said, "We can relax on this one."

"Sod that," Anthony said "I ain't leavin' this one to chance. Too much at stake for that. You sort the bugs out?"

"Yeah. Office and kitchen, but…"

"No buts. Any dodgy call Albert makes I wanna know. It'll ping my 'phone, right?"

"Yeah, but you won't be able to hear him."

"Don't matter, I'll see the number and know what to do. No drinking for you for the next twenty-four hours. Need you ready to go soon as I call. Then we can go over and sort this once and for all. I'll go see the doc next and get the necessary."

"Sort it? The doc? What? You mean Albert?"

Anthony nodded.

George stopped and stared. "Jesus, boss, that's big. You sure? Dunno if I could do that."

"You don't have to do nothin' 'cept drive me. The needle's all I need."

"Still an' all, boss, you sure about this?"

"Dead sure."

"But your old man said leave it."

"Did he? Did he really? You heard what he said to me at the end?" Anthony said.

"Yeah, course, said he'd 'ave a word and sort it," George said.

"Before that? You not get it?".

"No. Get what?"

Anthony smiled and shook his head. "Then you gotta learn to listen better, George, you wanna get anywhere in this business. "His heart'll do for him, I shouldn't wonder." You not hear that?"

"Well, yeah, I heard it, but he was just speculatin', yeah?"

"You don't know dad, it's the way he says things. That wasn't him thinking out loud, that was an instruction."

"Jesus! But Albert's his brother-in-law. He'd do that?"

"You really don't know dad, George my son. He's the most ruthless guy I've ever met. Anything gets in his way, threatens him, he sorts it. And I do mean sorts it. Whatever it takes."

George shook his head. "I'll look at him different from now on, that's for sure."

Eight

Albert barely responded to his wife's questions when he got home. After four or five grunts she put his dinner in front of him, poured his Pale Ale and left him alone.

He picked at his food and then sat at the table just staring at the wall. His mobile ringing startled him. He fumbled for it and put it to his ear without looking at the screen.

"Hello."

"Albert? It's Jack. Thought I'd give you a bell. Our Anthony's been round. Tells me you're a bit out of sorts, yeah? You alright?"

"Alright? No, I'm fucking not, Jack. Two firsts, in a day, at my age?"

"Two?"

"Yeah. First time I've ever seen a pile of dead bodies, first time I've topped a geezer. Thrown me right off it has."

"Yeah, I know, real sorry about that Albert, you shouldn't have been…"

"Jack. Don't. You don't do concern. It don't suit you."

"Point taken, Albert, but I'm still sorry about you having to do that fucking Pole."

"Not as sorry as me," Albert said. Y'know the worst thing? I never meant to at first, did I? Went to calm him down, stop him hittin' me. I gave him a smack, but he was still alive when I went to the truck. Weren't feeling all that well, admittedly, but he was still breathing. When I came back in though, I couldn't stop. Turned his head to pulp and broke every bone in his fucking body. But shakin' after. Never knew I had it in me, Jack."

Nor me, Jack thought. Nor me.

"I know Albert," he said. But we've all got it in us my old son, we just need the right trigger is all. You're lucky you never felt it before."

"Yeah, but our Anthony though, running straight round to you tell you. What's all that about, eh?"

"Don't be a prat, Albert. What else did you expect, eh? He would've told me anyway. You know that. And I would've been well pissed off if he hadn't. And he'd have to tell me how shaken you were. Couldn't leave that out, now could he?"

"Yeah, but givin' it to you about me as well, about all what I said. No need for that. I'd've told you meself."

"But what d'you want him to do, Albert? You talkin' bollocks about doin' something about it? Our business? Bound to worry him. Worries me as well. Told him though, Albert'll never say, never do, anything. Just the shock it was. Yeah?"

"Yeah, yeah. And o'course I wouldn't. Like I said to Anthony, just need a coupla days, sort it out in me head. Be alright in a couple."

"What I told him," Jack said.

"It's just this, the business Jack. What're we doin' in it? What're you doin' in it? I mean, we were okay back in the day, weren't we? Small time compared to some of 'em, but we did all right? Made a few quid."

"A few quid is right," Jack said. A few. But do you see any knock-off watches, toasters, tellys, and fridges round here, these days, Albert? See us driving round in dodgy second-hand motors? No, you don't. It was all we had back then. Everything knock-off. Scuffling to get the next load and shift it to the next lot of mugs. Making a few shillings but livin' hand to mouth basically. And yeah, I suppose we got by alright. But you know what it's like, Albert, stand still and you get eaten by some bigger firm. Then you go from getting by to having sod all. You gotta keep moving to stay alive. Like sharks. And that's what I did. Anthony's just doing the same thing. Only he's better at it than I ever was. One year of this, one more year Albert, and we can get out altogether. Off to Spain. Retire with the sun on our old bones."

"I can't stop thinking though, that could've been our girls, Jack."

Jack Foley took a deep breath while he controlled his temper. No point in losing it now. "Talk silly, Albert," he said in a calm, quiet voice. "Of course it couldn't. Our girls? That's bollocks. It could never be ours. We take care of 'em too well. We can afford to. And even if we couldn't, no way we'd be sellin' them on to filthy pervs, is there?"

There was a lengthy pause while each man thought about what he should say. And whether he dared say what he wanted to. Eventually, Albert just carried on the previous conversation.

"Afford to? By killing other young girls we can afford to look after ours? That what you mean?"

"Albert, Albert. How many bleedin' times. It was outside our control. A one-off. Not like it's a part of the business, is it?

But if we weren't in this business it never would have happened, Albert thought. "Maybe not, Jack," he said. "But why're we doin' it? You could stop it, you could. Can't you talk to Anthony?"

"I can't stop it, Albert, even if I wanted to. Not in it anymore, am I? Anthony runs it, you know that. I'm still head of this family, yeah, but not the firm. Not anymore. That's Anthony. He decides. Talks to me when he wants, gets my take on things, but he makes the decisions. That's how it is so get used to it Albert."

"Would you?" Albert asked, pointing a fat forefinger.

"Eh? Would I what?"

"You know what I mean, Jack. Would you have us in this business. Young girls an' all? Honestly now."

"You know I wouldn't, if I had a choice, Albert. I agree with you it's a dirty business. Them ponces with ten-year olds. Turns my bleedin' stomach it does. But it ain't the worst thing we've ever done." Jack paused. "And did Anthony tell you the numbers?" he asked.

"Yeah but…"

"No buts, Albert. Those numbers? That's us, our kids, and grandkids sorted. For life."

"I get that," Albert said, "I do. But Spain?"

"Yeah, it's time you went, Albert. And sharpish. There's a villa, pool, the lot. Plenty bars. You can watch Spurs in one of 'em. Got the whole Premier League over there."

"So. You dealin' the cards now Jack?"

"Well, stands to reason, Albert. My game, my deck, my deal."

"And a stacked deck, I bet," Albert said.

Jack laughed. "Not at all Albert. Not at all… but tell you what, you can shuffle 'em as many times as you like, but I deal 'em. Don't play any cards ain't in your hand, know what I'm saying?"

Albert sighed, giving in to the inevitable outcome. But inside he was dreading the thought of leaving his beloved London and moving to Spain. A painful thought for a man who had never lived more than two miles from the house in which he'd been born.

"Yeah," he said, "I s'pose. Don't want no more to do with this bleedin' business that's for sure. And if Spain gets me out of it well… okay. And Dor'll be well made up so there's one silver lining at least. When we talking?"

"Couple of days is all. Week at most. Use the Wilson passports. Sorry Albert, it really is my fault. Never should've involved you in this. So. You ain't gonna do anything silly are you? Told Anthony you wouldn't."

"Nah, not at all. I'm done with all this. Today finished it for me."

"Good. I'll let Anthony know. Settle his mind for him. Listen, why don't you go up West, shop for some holiday clothes, take Dor', give her your gold card, that'll make her even happier. How about that?"

"Yeah, could do," Albert said. "Sounds good. Like you say, Dor'll love it."

"And tell you what," Jack said, "why don't you come round tomorrow. We'll go for a couple of beers. Just you and me. And some lunch? You fancy Kelly's. Ain't been there in a while."

Albert was silent for a moment or two. "What's all this then, Jack? Us on pints of light and bitter and pie 'n' mash to follow? You doin' a memory lane trip on me, or what?"

"Yeah, why not? Do you the world of good. Forget the warehouse tomorrow. You and me'll have a walk, stroll in the manor, in the sunshine. See some old faces. Then a coupla beers, some grub and maybe a coupla more beers after. That suit you? We can sort out getting you and Dor' to Spain while we're at it. Yeah?"

"Sounds good," Albert said. "See you about eleven then?"

"Yea, see you then. And dress smart Albert. We'll put on a show for 'em."

"Yeah, best whistle, Jack. See you."

Nine

Just before she went to bed Doreen came into the room and sat down at the table. She took both his hands in hers.

"What is it, love? I ain't never seen you like this before."

Albert just shook his head and looked down at the table. Doreen looked at him but didn't know whether she should push him. Then decided, yes.

"Come on love. Somethin's really botherin' you. I know you. What is it?"

Albert looked up at her and shook his head again. "It's just business, Dor', nothin' really. Nothin' you need worry about anyway."

"Must be somethin', Albert," she said, "the mood you're in tonight. Can't help worrying because you're never like this normally. Even if thing's have gone wrong, you always know what to do to sort things. But you seem, I dunno, hopeless, helpless tonight. So come on, love, talk to me, tell me all about it."

"Ah, just some nonsense at work today is all. The warehouse. The trucks and stuff. Things were messed up, badly. Couldn't've been worse to be honest. And it weren't my fault, not down to me at all. But Jack seems to think it was, 'cos he's sending us off to Spain in a couple of days. Get me out of the way. Permanently."

Doreen smiled and inwardly thanked God.

"Oh! Well, you know what I think about that, love. I've been hoping we could go to Spain for ages now. Can't wait. But all that what happened today, it really wasn't your fault?"

"Nah, nothin' to do with me at all. I even helped sort it, but I still think Jack's blamin' me in a way."

"Then I'd look out for yourself, Albert, love," Doreen said.

"What you on about? Don't need to look after meself, do I? It's Jack. I know he shouldn't blame me for what happened, but Spain's okay. This time next month we'll be enjoyin' the sun and the pool and everything."

"I know, I know, but all I'm saying is you trust Jack a bit too much sometimes, love. You idolise him, you always have, but in the end all Jack cares about is himself and family."

"But I am family," Albert said.

"Yes, but only married into it," she said. "You're not blood. And you know Jack, blood's all that matters to him. So like I said, just don't you trust him too much Albert, love. You got to look after yourself a bit more."

"Now who's worrying too much," Albert said.

"Maybe, but I know my brother better'n anybody alive. I love him to bits, but I wouldn't trust him far as I could throw him where business is concerned. And neither should you, love. Don't be too long coming up, eh?" She kissed him on the forehead and went off upstairs to bed.

When he was sure she'd be safely tucked in, Albert stood up, put his mobile into his pocket and walked out of the house. He climbed into his car and drove back to the warehouse.

Everything had been cleared away. No sign that Peter, the trucks and the bodies, had ever existed. He let himself in and walked through to the office before he switched a light on. He sat at his desk, poured himself a large whisky and savoured the first mouthful. Then he checked his notebook, lifted the 'phone and punched in a number. It rang five times before being answered.

"DCI Clarke," he said.

Originally from Newcastle, Ian is now happily retired and living in Bristol. He has 'scribbled' all his life, mainly for the pleasure of friends and family, but has only recently begun writing full-time. His personal motto is: *"You're never too old and it's never too late."*

Drawn from his broad experience of life, the stories in this volume explore many of the aspects of hope. The experience of living with it, holding on to it and the dark pain of losing it. These ten stories are a final attempt to describe another essential part of the human condition.

This is the third book in the trilogy - "It's The Human Condition".

Printed in Great Britain
by Amazon